*Dear Diary,*

*If this is a dream, don't ever let me wake up!*

*Just when I was at my most desperate—when I truly believed I'd never find anyone to love—a tall dark stranger literally crashed into my life. (Okay, so it was me who crashed into his fender....)*

*I have to admit I was becoming a little discouraged, especially with my thirtieth birthday looming. It's been wonderful seeing Hannah and so many of my other friends find their soul mates. But inside, part of me was crying, "When is it my turn?"*

*And then came Nick. I honestly never believed that any man could make me feel this way, especially a bush pilot from the wilds of Alaska. The physical attraction was there from day one. I just look at that tall, rugged body and those soulful eyes, and my blood really does heat. When he touches me... Well, no way am I going to share that, even with my diary.*

*There's just one problem. Nick sees the relationship between a man and a woman in practical terms. He refuses to believe in love, maybe because there's been so little of it in his life.*

*But I can never marry someone who doesn't love me, body and soul.*

*Oh, Nick...don't let this chance slip away. You are my soul mate. I just know it. Let yourself love me the way I love you. I've waited too long to find you to let you walk away.*

*Till tomorrow,*

*Katherine*

## JILL SHALVIS

has been making up stories since she could hold a pencil. Now, thankfully, she gets to do it for a living, and doesn't plan to ever stop. She is the bestselling, award-winning author of over two dozen novels. She's hit the Waldenbooks bestseller lists, was a 2000 RITA® Award nominee and is a two-time National Reader's Choice Award winner. She was nominated for a *Romantic Times* Career Achievement Award in Romantic Comedy, Best Duets and Best Temptation, and writes series romance for both Silhouette and Harlequin.

# *Forrester Square*
## LEGACIES . LIES . LOVE .

# JILL SHALVIS
## COME FLY WITH ME

HARLEQUIN®

TORONTO • NEW YORK • LONDON
AMSTERDAM • PARIS • SYDNEY • HAMBURG
STOCKHOLM • ATHENS • TOKYO • MILAN • MADRID
PRAGUE • WARSAW • BUDAPEST • AUCKLAND

HARLEQUIN BOOKS
225 Duncan Mill Road, Don Mills,
Ontario, Canada M3B 3K9

ISBN 0-373-61277-X

COME FLY WITH ME

Jill Shalvis is acknowledged as the author of this work:

Visit us at www.eHarlequin.com

**Printed in U.S.A.**

Dear Reader,

I was so excited to get to be part of the FORRESTER SQUARE continuity project, and even more excited to dig into this story. Not just because of the setting (I love both Seattle and Alaska), but because of the depth and complexity of the characters, and the ongoing mystery of Forrester Square itself.

What's up for you in *Come Fly with Me?* Well, you have one strong, independent, warm and nurturing heroine looking for her happily ever after, and one tall, dark and slightly attitude-ridden hero looking for anything but. Poor Nick. He's just one of those guys who is so baffled and mystified by love, and I just got such a kick out of making him take the plunge. Hope you get a kick out of him, too.

Happy reading,

*Jill Shalvis*

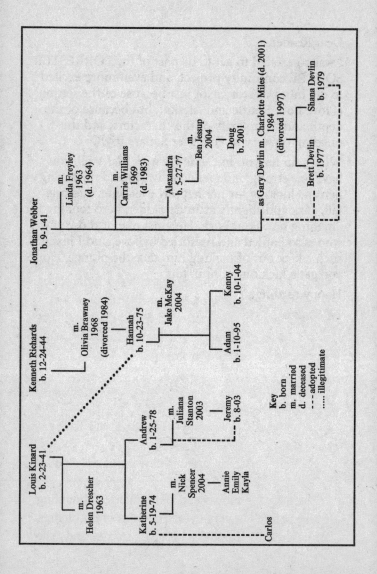

Louis Kinard
b. 2-23-41

m.
Helen Drescher
1963

Katherine
b. 5-19-74

m.
Nick
Spencer
2004

Annie
Emily
Kayla

Andrew
b. 1-25-78

m.
Juliana
Stanton
2003

Jeremy
b. 8-03

Carlos

Kenneth Richards
b. 12-24-44

m.
Olivia Brawney
1968
(divorced 1984)

Hannah
b. 10-23-75

m.
Jake McKay
2004

Adam
b. 1-10-95

Kenny
b. 10-1-04

Jonathan Webber
b. 9-1-41

m.
Linda Freyley
1963
(d. 1964)

m.
Carrie Williams
1969
(d. 1983)

Alexandra
b. 5-27-77

m.
Ben Jessup
2004

Doug
b. 2001

as Gary Devlin m. Charlotte Miles (d. 2001)
1984
(divorced 1997)

Brett Devlin
b. 1977

Shana Devlin
b. 1979

Key
b. born
m. married
d. deceased
- - adopted
...... illegitimate

# CHAPTER ONE

THE WEDDING MARCH BEGAN. A soft murmur of joy danced through the crowded pews of the church, and a hundred smiling faces turned to watch Katherine take her father's hand and start down the aisle.

Finally. How long had she waited for this, dreamed of it, fantasized… She was so excited, so elated that her heart threatened to burst right out of her chest. She'd pictured this scene so many times she could make the walk with her eyes closed, but no way was she going to miss a single moment. With a shaky inhale, smiling with all her being, she took her first step toward the rest of her life.

Her groom stood at the head of the aisle, tall, sure, kind…her every wish come true.

''Katherine,'' he whispered, reaching his hand toward her. ''My love, my life.''

He was everything she'd ever wanted, and waiting for her.

But then the crowd suddenly changed, doubling in size before her very eyes. The front of the church, lit only with candles, became fuzzy, and she couldn't see her husband-to-be. Panic filled her, and her breathing quickened.

*Just relax,* she told herself. He was there, and tonight he'd give her what she'd craved all her adult life.

A baby. Her very own baby.

Everything she'd ever wanted was so close now, just within her reach. But as she made her way down the aisle, the fog seemed to thicken, blocking her way to the front of the church.

How had fog gotten in the church? As she watched in horror, the tall, proud form of her groom shimmered and started to fade.

"No!" She struggled to run toward him, but the heavy silk of her long dress weighed her down, and the high-heeled sandals she'd put on only a few minutes before turned to lead boots. She screamed for him. "Come back! Please, come back!"

"Katherine…"

The fog surrounded her now, blocking her view entirely. Suddenly, his outstretched hand came through, and she leaped at it.

*Yes!* She felt his fingers…as they slipped through her grasp.

No! She wanted this, wanted him, wanted their baby… With a gasping sob, she threw herself toward him, flying through the air—

And woke up sitting in her own bed with the alarm blaring. Her legs were tangled in her soft, flowered sheets, her hands fisted at her sides, her body covered in a fine sheet of perspiration.

Just a dream, just a horrible, horrible dream. A nightmare. Katherine hit the snooze button, plopped to her back, and waited for her breathing to return to normal.

It took a while. "This is ridiculous," she told the ceiling.

And embarrassing. Every night, the same thing, waking up unfulfilled and longing and…achy. It had to stop. Her life was good, for God's sake. As one of three owners of Forrester Square Day Care, she got to do her favorite thing for a living—work with children. Being in charge also gave her a flexibility and a freedom she loved and craved.

And okay, so she also enjoyed the control, but she'd worked hard to get where she was. She had everything she needed—a family she loved very much, friends who cared about her and Carlos, her foster child, a boy near and dear to her heart.

She truly had everything she could ever want.

So why did she still have the dream every night? It didn't take a psychologist to understand. Yes, she *appeared* to have everything—except the love of her life and a child of her own.

Turning her head, she eyed the pamphlets on her nightstand, the ones from the sperm bank she'd recently contacted. She'd be turning thirty soon, and with no prospective husband—even the men in her dreams vanished every night—she'd decided to rely on herself. If she couldn't have the whole "family" package, a husband and a baby of her own, then she'd settle for what she could have. Just the baby.

She showered, dressed and fixed breakfast before she went down the hall toward Carlos's bedroom. She didn't have far to go. Her house was a very small cottage, *small* being the operative word here. She could hardly turn around in her hallway without bumping her elbows on the walls.

But she loved her quiet, quaint neighborhood, and had sunk her heart and soul into the house. She had lots of windows, and a window box for each, filled with colorful flowers she grew herself.

From the living room and bedroom windows she could see the tall, majestic snow-capped Cascades east of Seattle, a view that had sealed the deal when she'd first seen the place. On a clear day—not this morning—she could see "the Mount," the term locals fondly called Mt. Rainier.

The interior of her house always reminded her of spring. Soft colors, light wood flooring, big comfy furniture that invited one to curl up on it, which she did whenever she found the time to do so. She had a thing for chintz, as well as mementos, each with its own sentimental value. There were photos from her childhood of her father, her mother, her brother...friends. She'd added many of Carlos now that he'd become such a part of her life. A home after her own heart.

*And it should be enough.*

What did it say about her that it wasn't, that something was missing, that she needed more?

Just inside Carlos's room, she softly whispered his name. The thirteen-year-old sat straight up, then blinked twice in slow succession, looking like an owl at the crack of dawn.

The poor baby wasn't a morning person, and no matter how happy he was here with her, how remarkably well adjusted, for a beat every single morning when she first called his name, panic would race across his features.

Then he would remember, and that too would show on his face—each emotion as he felt it. He no longer lived on the streets, he lived with her, where he had food and shelter and clothes and all the love and affection he wanted.

"Hey, baby." She came forward and rumpled his already rumpled hair, knowing that her touch, her voice would help bring him back. "Just me."

His smile was slow and sweet and full of enough relief to tug at her hard. He wasn't her first foster kid, but she wanted him to be her last. She wanted to adopt him, and in fact had been working with his social worker toward that very event.

"For a sec, I forgot...." He trailed off and lifted a bony shoulder.

"I know. You okay?"

He shot her a brave smile that broke her heart. She had no idea how she could love him so much already, but she did, and once Katherine loved, it was for life. She'd fight like a momma bear to protect him and make him hers.

"If you hurry," she said, "I've got waffles for you before school."

"With strawberries?" He was already tossing aside his covers and leaping to his feet. Any lingering sleepiness always vanished at the promise of food.

That he was so easy to please only made her all the more determined to spoil him. "With strawberries," she confirmed.

"And whipped cream?"

"Not for breakfast."

"Aw, man. Just a bite?"

"Nope," she said cheerfully, and headed to the door. "See you in the kitchen when you're cleaned up and dressed."

He met her there in less than three minutes, so she had to doubt he'd spent much time on the cleaning-up part, but he smelled like toothpaste and his hair had been gelled—this was apparently extremely important to boys his age—so she figured he would hit everything else later that night with a required shower.

She watched him dig into the waffles, then turned

to the window over the sink. It was raining. No big surprise. This was, after all, Seattle, and the city wasn't called Lady Gray for nothing. But she loved stormy weather, and especially these warm spring storms. They were good for her garden.

She dropped Carlos off at school with only a slight sigh for his too loose pants and the slouch he purposely put into his stance as he exited the car.

Then she drove to work, parking as close as she could get. Still a little bit haunted by her dream, by the fact she had an appointment at the sperm bank this afternoon, by…well, life, she beelined to Caffeine Hy's.

It was a daily stop.

The little coffee shop was located just on the east side of her day care, on the bottom floor of a historical sandstone office building. On warmer days there were outdoor tables and chairs on the sidewalk, but this morning they were stacked against the wall, not yet set up.

Desperate for caffeine, she stepped inside, shook loose the rain from her hair and was immediately surrounded by the familiar, delicious scent of coffee.

Hy's was done up in a rather bohemian style, with mismatched chairs in a variety of seating arrangements, wooden chairs clustered around a scarred old table, upholstered chairs grouped around a low coffee table. The walls were deep mustard and apricot, and the interior lighting was dim, provided by an old beaded floor lamp and paper, wall sconces. A variety of scarves and cloths in all different textures and fabrics were scalloped across the ceiling, along with original origami figures done by any number of talented, steady customers as they sipped their coffee.

The walls were lined with shelves of coffee beans. Soft music, laughter and talking filled the air. Inhaling deeply, she headed directly for the thankfully short line. For a moment she studied the menu handwritten on the chalkboard, but she knew she was going to get her favorite, a regular cappuccino, so she casually perused the crowd, her heart already starting to beat just a little heavier.

He was here, he had to be…yep. There. At the counter. He was a perfect stranger, really, but she'd seen him three mornings running now.

He leaned negligently against the far end of the granite counter with his own cup of java. His head was bent, engrossed in the *Seattle Times*. His dark hair was long, curling slightly around the collar of his overshirt, and at least a few days' worth of stubble covered his lean jaw. He wore black from head to toe: black T-shirt beneath an open black flannel shirt, stretched over broad shoulders, black Levi's and black work boots that both looked well worn, assuring her his *Outsider* look was natural rather than posed. His long legs were stretched out in that soft-looking denim, past the next bar stool, which was empty. His arms extended alongside the paper, his large body taking up more than his allowed space. As he had for three mornings now, he exuded a muscled power that sort of simmered off him, and she had trouble looking away.

He glanced up, and unerringly landed his dark, piercing gaze right on her.

Katherine jerked her gaze from him. Stupid, stupid, stupid, getting caught staring at him like a silly teen. Trying to cool her hot cheeks, she concentrated on the conversation around her, on the music, on the scent of desperately needed coffee, but utterly unable to help herself, she eventually drew in another breath and took just one more peek.

He was still looking at her.

In fact, he studied her from head to toe with unabashed curiosity, taking in her comfortable walking sandals, her flowing gauzy skirt, which was her favorite because it never needed an iron, her long-sleeved, scooped-neck T-shirt in the same peach color, her dark hair, which she'd left loose and hanging down her back because her best clip was on her desk at the day-care center.

She tried to work up some annoyance or outrage at being so thoroughly checked out, but she didn't feel annoyance or outrage.

She felt…a little tingly.

"Ma'am?"

She realized it was her turn to place her order,

and that the poor server had been trying to get her attention for the past few seconds. More than a little unnerved, she ordered. Then she dropped her change, and then her keys as well.

She was just tired, she decided. And her behavior a little juvenile because of it. That explained getting distracted by a handsome man, which wasn't surprising when she thought about it. She spent so much of her life in nurturing mode, as dictated by her job and personality. It wasn't often she let other aspects of herself come to the surface. But they were coming to the surface now, namely an odd and new sexuality that made her think maybe she needed a good, hot romance to read tonight.

She waited for her cappuccino, thinking the temperature in the room had shot up in the past few moments, and she wondered if her stranger felt the same way, as if he needed ice water instead of coffee. She pictured him standing up to his full height—which had to be impressive—and ordering a cup of ice to go.

The thought only made her hotter.

When her coffee was ready, she took it and turned back around, actually holding her breath with anticipation. Would he smile? Would he stand up? Introduce himself?

Or just grab her and kiss her senseless—

He'd gone back to his paper.

Yep, she was hot all right. So hot he'd forgotten all about her.

Oh well, what had she expected? To be swept off her feet? And then what? Ask him if he had good swimmers? Ha! Smiling at the ridiculous thought of him being her private sperm bank, she headed for the door, minding her precious caffeine with a careful hand. No wonder she needed a sperm bank. She couldn't even get a guy to flirt with her, much less date her.

Enjoying the feel of the morning, she walked next door to Forrester Square Day Care. The Belltown area was upscale and rather expensive, but she had a benefactor who'd lent her a sizable sum of money to start up, and being the old friend of the family that he was, Jordan Edwards had insisted he do so without interest. Every day Katherine walked through here and thought of him and his generosity, and silently thanked him again.

The Belltown district, which was not far from Queen Anne Hill, where she'd spent the early years of her childhood, had been her first choice for the business, and Hannah and Alexandra, her business partners and oldest friends, were as thrilled with the area as she was. Their building was sandstone brick, like the one that housed Caffeine Hy's, with large front windows filled with the seasonal flowers she grew at home. Her need to garden amused those around her, but growing and nurturing things was a part of her. On the west side of the day care sat The Grey Gallery, an upscale gallery and museum featuring local artists, making it a popular destination for tourists.

She opened the gate and walked up the path, passing the wrought-iron park benches she'd picked up for a song to match the half fence enclosing the front yard. Hanging from the roof of the building was a huge banner in the shape of a house, complete with peaked roof and smoking chimney, proudly displaying their name in a child's handwriting.

Forrester Square Day Care.

As always, she got a warm fuzzy feeling just entering the front door. She was the first to arrive, and unlocked the place. Generally the three of them, Hannah, Alexandra and herself, took turns opening and closing. It wasn't her turn this morning, it should have been Hannah's, but Hannah, several months pregnant, had been instructed by her doctor to work at home for a couple of weeks.

Katherine didn't mind—most of the time she came early, anyway. She liked to be the first to arrive and enjoyed opening the place up. Flipping on the lights and the fun kiddie music, watering her plants. Just standing in the middle of the events room, which was their main space downstairs for gathering, gave her a warm fuzzy feeling, knowing how far they'd come, and how many kids they provided a home for during the day.

But…there was no doubt, something was missing. Something inside her. All her life she'd been the responsible one, and after her father had been sent to prison when Katherine was only nine, her mother, Helen, had returned to teaching, often leaning on Katherine to do the mothering to her younger brother, Drew. Besides that and school, Katherine had eventually taken over most of the cooking and caring for the house, as well.

She'd done it all, without a single regret, and somehow, over the years, caring for those around her had become her life. That hadn't changed, even though her father was home from prison and her brother was married. And now she had the day care, where she was the driving force behind a successful business that kept many friends employed and even more kids happy.

But…another *but* today!…ever since Hannah and Jack's wedding last month, she'd been feeling sad. Unsettled. As if she'd lost a part of herself.

Darn it, she wanted a family of her own; a husband to love and kids to mother. Fostering Carlos went a long way in filling her heart, and so did the children she saw every day, but she needed more.

She thought of the sexy stranger in the coffee shop and the way her body reacted. Her hormones had definitely revved.

And yet she was going to a sperm bank today.

Had she really given the single men out there a

fair shot? She did tend to keep herself so busy she rarely had time for socializing, much less husband searching.

Hmm. She'd absolutely come to terms with having a baby without a husband, but... Deep, deep down she still wanted it all—the romance, the lover, the friend to turn to in the middle of the night....

"Hey." Alexandra walked into the room. "You beat me again. I thought you were going to stop doing it all." She laughed. "*What am I saying?* You can't help yourself."

At twenty-six, Alexandra was just a few years younger than Katherine. She had short red hair, moss-green eyes and fair, flawless skin that never needed makeup. Katherine, Hannah and Alexandra had spent the early years of their childhood together. Their fathers had been business partners in Eagle Aerotech, a company that specialized in computer software for airplanes, until tragedy tore their lives apart. Katherine's father was sent to prison for embezzlement and selling sensitive computer software on the black market, and Alexandra's parents were both killed when their house burned. While these events strained their parents' friendships, the three girls had forged a bond of sisterhood that couldn't be broken, even when Alexandra was sent to live with relatives in Montana.

In fact, when Alexandra returned to Seattle the previous fall, she had lived with Katherine, who'd been happy to mother her friends. But as a free spirit and a wanderer who needed to be alone more often than not, Alexandra had soon found her own place.

Katherine still missed her, but understood Alexandra needed her space in a way neither Katherine nor Hannah ever had. Today her friend's face looked a little wan and pale, making Katherine take a closer look. In Alexandra's eyes was a worry that brought out the same in Katherine. "Honey, what's the matter?"

Alexandra lifted a shoulder. "Nothing. I'm fine."

"It's something." Katherine crossed the room and took Alexandra's hand. "Talk to me. Is it Gary?"

Gary was the homeless man who'd been hanging around the day care. Sweet, kind, terribly thin and often confused, he had such a gentleness of spirit, he'd eventually become a favorite among the center's employees, all of whom took turns bringing him food and chatting with him.

But it was Alexandra who'd been drawn to the man first. Recently she'd even tried to help him figure out his past, which he couldn't remember clearly.

"No." Alexandra hung up her sweater and sighed. "It's Griff." Griffin Frazier, a policeman, was her on-again, off-again boyfriend. "He…" She rolled her eyes. "He wants to take the relationship to the 'next level.'"

Ah, the kiss of death, since Alexandra didn't do the "next level" well. Commitment was a bad word in her book. "What are you going to do?"

"Break up." She sighed again, but when she turned around she smiled, her first of the day. "You know what? Sad as it is, just saying it makes me feel better."

Katherine smiled. If that wasn't the difference between them right there. Alexandra couldn't handle ties, Katherine craved them. "Then it's right."

"Yeah." She squeezed Katherine's hand. "And anyway, thanks for listening. So, now tell me why *you're* frowning."

"Because I just remembered I have a call to make."

"The sperm bank?"

"I need another day."

"What you need is a cancellation, Katherine. You're not ready—"

"I'm ready, just…another day." She smiled as she lifted her shoulder. "I'll be right back."

She went into the office the three of them shared. There were more windows here, with healthy, glowing plants, bright-colored walls and three large desks. Alexandra's was a disaster zone, Hannah's was bare bones, and Katherine's had nice, tidy stacks. It always made her laugh, how different they were, but she didn't stop to laugh now.

She went straight to her desk and dialed the sperm

bank. "This is Katherine Kinard," she said when the receptionist answered.

"Hello, Katherine."

She winced. It was the same receptionist she'd talked to yesterday.

And the day before. "I'd like to c—"

"Let me guess." The receptionist had a wry tone to her voice. "You want to cancel your appointment."

"Postpone." Katherine bit her lip. "I'm sorry, I'm being a pest. I know."

"Don't worry about it. You've only called to re-schedule...what? Three times? Four?" The woman laughed gently. "Some call twenty or thirty times, so don't give it another thought. This is truly a very big decision, we understand that."

But she wanted a baby so much. "Can I come tomorrow instead?"

"Well..."

"I'll be ready tomorrow," Katherine said quickly. "Really."

"I believe that *you* think you will, but...honestly? My office manager disagrees."

"I'll be there," she said firmly.

"I have an idea. Why don't you give yourself a little longer than that? Say...a couple of weeks."

"No, really." Katherine opened her calendar and put a star on tomorrow's square. In red. She had no husband in sight, not so much as a date, and her biological clock was ticking.

She wanted a baby. "I'll be ready tomorrow," she vowed.

"You're *sure?*"

"Very." Katherine hung up the phone and tried to put it out of her mind, but the conversation stayed in her head all day.

She *was* sure she wanted a baby, that she could do it all by herself.

So why did her restlessness follow her like a shadow?

## CHAPTER TWO

KATHERINE HAD the wedding dream again that night, only this time she made it all the way down the aisle and out of the church. She and the love of her life had a house, a white picket fence, a minivan and babies; beautiful, sweet babies that brought so much joy to her heart it physically hurt when she woke up and found herself hot, achy and alone.

Again, she plopped onto her back and studied the ceiling. "This is getting old," she said, and rolled out of bed.

After the warm, joyous dream, the sperm bank pamphlets on her nightstand mocked her with their impersonal manner of getting children.

At first she'd been so sure going this route to get pregnant would feel right, but where was the certainty now? She was a well rounded, educated, sensible individual. Not naive by any stretch. If she had doubts—which apparently she did—she knew she needed to listen to them.

The biggest doubt, the one that wouldn't go away, was telling her she needed more than a baby. She needed a real-life romance, with a kind, sensitive, loving man who'd make her his reason for living. Her own Prince Charming.

She shouldn't, couldn't, settle for less.

Carlos poked his head into her bedroom and gave her a wide grin. "I can't believe I beat you out of bed for once."

"Just tell me you saved me some hot water."

"I didn't use any."

Of course not. What was it about boys and showers anyway?

"But I did make breakfast."

"I knew I loved you for a reason." She climbed out of bed and gave him a big hug, thrilled when his arms lifted to come around her as well. For so long he hadn't liked to be touched, but now here he was, hugging her back, without the slightest sign of embarrassment or discomfort.

*There.* There was some cause for real elation and joy.

"I put a lot of hard work into breakfast," he said proudly, leading her down the hall. "Come on. Come look and see."

Katherine couldn't wait. Up until now, he'd taken little interest in cooking. "What did you come up with?"

"Close your eyes."

When she did so, Carlos led her into the kitchen. "Okay."

Katherine opened her eyes.

On the table sat a bowl of cold cereal and milk. She burst out laughing at his "hard work," and so did he.

"I'll pour," he said, and when she sat, he poured her milk.

"This is nice." She leaned over to kiss him. "Thank you."

"It's kinda like we're a—" Going a little red, he sat down and started shoving food into his mouth.

"Like we're a…what?"

"Nothing."

"Like we're a family?" She reached out to touch his rigid arm. "Is that what you mean?"

"Yeah." He lifted a shoulder. "Stupid."

"No, it isn't." Reaching over, she hugged him again. "I love being a family with you. So much." And it should be enough. She wanted it to be.

But as much as she loved him, she still needed more.

SHE SPENT the morning helping Marilyn Aibee with the four-year-olds. They finger painted, worked on sharing issues, read some of her favorite books. By lunchtime she was finally smiling from her heart.

Eating at her desk, she talked to her mother, who sounded good. She also checked in with Drew, her brother. He sounded so happy and in love since he'd married Julia and adopted her baby son. Katherine had hired her sister-in-law to work with the infants at Forrester Square, where Julia was a real asset.

Katherine's heart relaxed even more. Yes, life was good. It was. She'd made it so.

But behind all her happy thoughts was the one regarding her appointment after work. The sperm bank, the place that could give her what she'd wanted for so long…

And yet, she knew the truth. What was missing from her life couldn't be fixed by bringing a baby into this world alone.

Nope. She couldn't go through with it after all, but after dealing with her for so long, and being so kind about it, the people at the clinic—especially the saint of a receptionist—deserved a personal visit to explain.

She left work a little early for the appointment she wasn't going to keep. She smelled a bit like the cookies one rambunctious cutie had had on his hands when he'd hugged her, and her hair had never managed to get up into its clip again. There was no one to care about her appearance, though, so she didn't worry about it.

One thing the earlier hour gave her was light traffic. Good thing, seeing as her mind wasn't entirely on the road. Maybe it was knowing she wasn't going to go through with her plans to have a baby on her own. Maybe it was her imminent birthday, signaling the start of a new decade that started with a big fat *three*.

Whatever, she wasn't going to let it get to her. Nope. She was going to enjoy her very nice life. She was going to be happy with that very nice life.

She clicked on her signal in anticipation of turning right up ahead, where she'd merge into traffic and drive out of the Belltown district. There was her favorite bookstore, another coffee shop… She considered stopping for a caffeine fix. She glanced inside, saw no line, and…and at the last minute saw the new four-way stop sign on the street where she'd previously only had to merge. *When had that gone up?*

With a bit of panic now, she glanced at the red Jeep in front of her, the one that had followed the law and had indeed stopped—was *still* stopped. She stomped on the brakes, wincing because she knew.

She wasn't going to stop in time.

In seemingly slow motion, she calculated her options. She couldn't veer to the right—there was no room with the parked cars along the sidewalk. She couldn't veer to the left without slamming into another car going even faster than she was.

She could do nothing but watch as she slid— *crunch!*—into the back of the Jeep.

Utter silence.

She took stock. She'd managed to slow to about ten miles per hour, so it hadn't quite rocked her world the way she'd expected, but the impact had jarred her enough that she felt her bones rattle.

It was a rather odd sensation to look out the windshield and see life as it had looked only a second ago, with the exception of her bumper having hit the bumper in front of her.

The driver's door to the Jeep opened. A long denim-clad leg materialized.

She blinked again, trying to focus with the sun beaming through her window, but all she could catch was his outline. Logically she knew she should get out of the car and make sure he was okay, but the *he* in question had already climbed out of the Jeep. He was a huge hulk of a man, and now that he'd fully emerged, she could make out his broad shoulders and powerful-looking arms as he stepped toward her. She swallowed hard.

Her fantasy man, the one haunting her dreams every night.

Then he opened her door and looked down at her with a frown. The sun was behind him now, and she squinted up at a pair of mirrored aviator sunglasses.

Had she hit her head? Logically she knew her fantasy groom couldn't be standing there staring down at her. Surely she'd simply conjured him up out of the blue—

"Are you all right?" His voice was low and husky, and just as sexy as it had been last night, and the night before, but there was an edge to it, a concerned edge. His hair was slightly darker, and longer than her groom's, but—

"Can you hear me?" As he spoke, he hunkered down at her side, his frown deepening as he ignored the few honks and the cars around them. Reaching up, his leather bomber jacket crinkling, he shoved his sunglasses on top of his head, presumably to eye her better, but it made her gasp.

So did the way he settled his big, warm hand on her shoulder.

And suddenly she realized. He wasn't her dream lover, but the man from the coffee shop, the mysterious stranger with the dark, piercing eyes, the one who'd caught her staring at him. "Oh my," she whispered, and let out a nervous laugh. "You'd never guess who I thought you were— Never mind. I'm just so sorry—" She craned her neck over the hood of her car. "I can't believe I didn't notice that new stop sign. Well, yes, maybe I can believe it, since I've been so preoccupied, which is no excuse." She turned back to him, nerves bubbling and making her mouth run on. "Are you okay?"

"Yes."

"Good." She shoved back her hair. "That's the last time I drive while thinking about thirtieth birthdays and sperm bank appointments, I'll tell you that." She shook her head. "I should have just canceled on the phone and been done with it." Realizing she was babbling horrifyingly personal details in her anxiety, she bit her lip. "Don't listen to me, okay? In fact, pretend I didn't say a word yet." She let out a laugh and buried her face in her hands. "Except for the part where I said sorry."

A *beep-beep-beep* had her lifting her head.

Her perfect stranger had pulled out his cell phone, and with an even deeper frown, was punching numbers.

"Wait." She put her hand on his fingers. "Don't call 9-1-1, I'm fine. *Really*," she insisted when she saw his doubtful expression. Her voice rose as a large truck rumbled by. "I just talk a little fast when I'm upset, that's all. Ignore me." She took a deep breath and stepped out of the car to prove how fine she was. But to get out, she had to brush against him.

There wasn't a single inch of give in that big, powerful body, not a one. The man had to top a minimum of six foot four, and was solid as a rock from head to toe. No excess fat on this guy. There was no fat at all.

"I think you should sit," he said.

Traffic was picking up, thanks to the lane they blocked. It moved around them for the most part, the Seattleites taking it all in stride with a typical mind-your-own-business attitude.

Which meant that even in a sea of people, she was virtually alone with this very large, very unhappy man who probably gobbled up negligent drivers for breakfast. "I'm so sorry." She moved toward the front of her car. Her bumper was indeed embedded in his. "I have insurance, good insurance," she promised. "I'll make sure everything is taken care of—"

He took her elbow in his hand and turned her back to face him. For such a big man, he had an incredibly gentle touch, but there was nothing gentle in his gaze. Those amazing eyes of his—annoyed, worried, frustrated, take your pick—searched her face very carefully. "Seriously," he said. "I want you to sit back down."

"I told you, I'm fine."

Ignoring that, he backed her to the curb and applied a firm pressure to her arms until she sat. Again he squatted in front of her. "How many fingers?" he asked, wriggling two in her face.

"I didn't hit my head." She tugged at her skirt, grateful she'd worn a dark denim one today, long enough so that she wasn't flashing him, and tough enough to withstand sitting on the sidewalk. She bought most of her clothes based on toughness, since working with preschoolers was as messy a job as they came. "Look, I let my thoughts run away with my good sense," she said. "And I'm terribly sorry, but I'm fine."

"Hmm." He studied her closely. "You don't look like you're going into shock."

"Because I'm not." She smiled.

He didn't.

Did he ever? His jaw was still lean, and still un-shaven. Tense. In fact, a muscle ticked in it.

*Her* fault. "I'm just so sorry. Like I said, I wasn't paying enough attention to the road because—" She broke off when he shook his head.

"If we're back to the sperm bank thing," he said, "I really don't need to hear it." He stood but didn't move away. His eyes were sharp on her, as if he were still asessing her for delayed shock or injuries. "You're sure you're not hurt."

In a completely inappropriate chain of thought, his concern caused an odd sort of shiver to race through her. If she *had* been hurt, what would he have done? If she had needed consoling…would he have wrapped those long, powerful arms around her? Used that amazing voice to soothe her nerves?

And why was she thinking this way? "I'm quite sure, thanks."

"Good." He looked extremely relieved, and fi-nally backed away. "Let's just exchange insurance information and I'll be off."

Right. He'd be off. Fast as he could get away from her. She might have laughed, though he'd likely call 9-1-1 again. He wasn't her fantasy man, which meant he was a guy. A real one. He didn't want to have any more conversation than was strictly necessary.

Of course not.

Standing, she went to the passenger side of her car and reached in for her purse. Pulling out a pad of paper that had only one sheet left on it, a sheet that was half scribbled over with various notes she'd made for herself then ignored, she ripped off the clean portion. She had a moment where she couldn't find her pen, but that was nothing new. She did have a red crayon. With it, she scribbled down her work phone number and address, then her insurance information.

Holding it out to him, she said, "I'm really so sorry. Why don't you give me your phone number so I can make sure this is all covered with a minimum of trouble for you?"

"The car is a rental. I purchased insurance, so it's not a problem."

He wasn't a local.

Before she could comment on that fact, he'd taken her elbow again and led her back to the driver's side of her car. At five foot nine and a half, she was taller than the average woman, and in her life had often felt like an Amazon next to men.

Not this man. Next to him she felt…petite. Dainty.

Feminine.

Oh boy. Overactive hormone alert.

"See if it starts," he said, and she was sure he didn't mean her inner engine.

In any case, just like her insides, her car started, no problem.

"Put it in reverse," he demanded, and she did.

"Back up a foot or two, slowly."

She managed that as well, thinking that for such an incredibly masculine, overtly sexy guy, he was awfully bossy.

"Good."

The one-word compliment felt like a volume coming from him, the apparent king of one-word answers, and silly as it seemed, she was glad she'd done something right in his opinion.

Without hesitation, he then straightened to his full height, which was quite impressive alone, even without the lean, sinewy bulk of him, and stepped into traffic now beginning to pile up a bit.

As he did, he held up his hand with all the authority of a traffic cop.

Katherine gaped. "Hey, wait. You can't just—"

People stopped.

He turned his head and glanced at her, clearly expecting her to just drive away.

But…just driving away meant…just driving away.

She didn't want to go yet, not when she hadn't taken a good look at his Jeep. She hadn't taken a good long look at him to make sure he wasn't hurt in any way, even though he'd claimed to be just fine, and he certainly looked pretty damn fine.

Maybe what she really felt upset about was the fact she hadn't gotten his name, hadn't found out why he was visiting, and whom, and how long he was staying.

Or where.

She hadn't...

"Go," he commanded, obviously more than happy to see her drive off into the sunset without a backward glance, reminding her he was most definitely not the hero of her dreams.

He wanted her to just drive away.

Never see him again. Sure, that was the logical thing. But... "*But—*"

"Go," he said again, and didn't look back.

Right. Go. And with another sigh, go she did.

## CHAPTER THREE

NICK SPENCER missed Alaska. He missed the wide open space, the clear, brisk air that felt so good in his lungs, the isolation, the spectacular beauty of the mountain peaks and vast wilderness...all of it.

He supposed some might say Seattle had its own beauty, with its unique architecture and interesting culture, and there was some truth to that.

If one was a city rat.

But he'd never been a city rat.

With everything he was, he yearned to just pack up and head home. His reason for coming here in the first place had fallen through, and though he could just get back in his plane and go, Steve had promised to try to come up with an alternative plan.

Nick doubted he could, but he'd give his old friend a few more days.

For now, he just had one errand to run. Looking up at the banner hanging from the large sandstone building, he read the child's handwriting: Forrester Square Day Care.

He glanced down at the paper in his hands, the

one with the writing in red crayon he'd received yesterday. Yep, he had the right place.

It was a few minutes after six so he was relieved to find the door still unlocked. Someone was working late, hopefully the person he needed to see. Katherine Kinard, the woman with the unusually soft doe-brown eyes, runaway mouth with the kissable lips and the woefully inadequate driving skills.

As he entered the center, he heard her voice. It was a soft, lyrical voice, he'd give her that. And while he recognized the book she was reading out loud, he doubted the author had intended for his words to sound so sweet and unbearably sexy at the same time.

"I'm going to eat you up," she read, and a young child laughed.

Nick did too, at himself, because the words conjured up quite a different picture in his mind from that of the child's, he was quite certain.

Something about the place, either the spacious, airy hallway lined with cheerful drawings, or the scent of paints and cookies, reminded him of home with the force of a kick to the gut.

God, he missed his kids.

Stepping farther inside, he moved toward her voice, down the hallway to the second door on the left. It was open to a large room decorated for kids, where he found her sitting on a giant bean bag by the far windows. A young boy sat on her lap holding the book *The Wild Thing,* looking as enraptured as Nick himself felt.

He already knew Katherine Kinard to be tall and willowy. That she talked too much when she was nervous. And that she had a face not so much classically beautiful as…arresting. He already knew her shiny, silky chestnut-brown hair fell to just past her shoulders, perfectly parted on the side. He already knew that she had creamy, smooth skin and unbelievably expressive eyes. But what he hadn't known, and what grabbed him by the throat now, was the way she looked smiling down at a child, with warmth and affection lighting her features, turning her into the most beautiful woman he'd ever seen.

She glanced up at the sound of his booted feet crossing the floor, and the expression that danced across her features wasn't exactly flattering. Tension. And a little fear to go with it.

Damn. Not exactly what he'd meant to inspire. "Evening," he said lightly, stopping where he was. The sooner he got out of here the better. "I just wanted to tell you I've paid for the damage to the rental car." He held up a hand when she started to get to her feet. "No, it's okay, don't get up. I just wanted you to know I'd done it so you don't run it through your insurance company and get your rates jacked up."

In spite of his words, she set aside the child and stood. She wore a soft, forest-green turtleneck with a matching long jumper. Her feet were bare, which made him want to smile for some odd reason. Obviously she dressed for comfort and ease of movement rather than to appeal to the male eye, but somehow, in that dress that so effectively hid her shape, she appealed anyway.

The kid on the floor held up his hands in the universal and silent demand to be picked up. Reading the language of a child effortlessly, Katherine Kinard did exactly that.

The front door opened again, and a couple came into the room. "I'm so sorry we're late!" The woman rushed forward, arms out.

"No problem." Katherine let the squirming boy down. He was grinning from ear to ear.

*"Mommy!"* Pumping his short legs across the floor, he threw himself at his mom, then shot a grin over his shoulder. "Bye!" he yelled to Katherine.

"Bye, Tommy, see you tomorrow."

"Bill me for the extra time," his mother said, hugging Tommy close. "And thanks again."

"You're very welcome." Katherine waved the family off. Then, giving Nick an inscrutable glance, she moved out of the big room and toward the front door, beyond which they could both see the street and the cars winding their way home on this rainy and quickly getting dark night.

"Let me get my checkbook from my office," she said. "I'll just reimburse you for your costs—"

"Wait." He came forward as she moved again, and caught her with a hand to her wrist. "That's just it. I don't want your money."

She stared down at his hand on her. Oh yes, she had a very interesting face, one that showed her every thought. And what she was thinking about now was possibly punching him.

Then she looked up. Granted, she had to tip her head back to do so, but she appeared to like making eye contact.

He had no idea why that was a turn-on.

She dragged her lower lip across her teeth.

Another turn-on.

It interested him she wore little makeup, and that her long hair flowed loose and slightly messy. It interested him a lot, since that meant she wasn't a woman hung up on her appearance.

Another extremely appealing trait, if he was counting, which apparently he was.

"I'm hoping," she said, "that I haven't been a completely stupid female by letting you in here." She eyed his hand on her wrist, which looked large and tanned and extremely male against her creamy, feminine skin. "And that you didn't come here to tear me limb from limb, or—"

"No." Christ, was he *that* scary? He'd think so, judging by the way his week had gone. Four days ago, his date had ditched him in the restaurant.

And now here was this woman, staring at him as

if he planned to eat her up for dessert. "Look, I just wanted to tell you about the Jeep."

"Thank you," she said very softly, and took a step back from him. "But I'd really feel better if you'd let me pay you. How much was it?"

"Nothing. And how about I promise not to tear you limb from limb so you can relax."

She let out a shaky smile. "Well, that'd be nice."

"Okay, then." He shoved a hand through his hair in frustration. "This is why I hate the city, I'm not great at the social thing. Let's start over."

"Good plan." She thrust her hand out. "Katherine Kinard. Annoying driver."

"Nick Spencer, annoying victim." He watched her lips quirk and he reached out for her hand, feeling a little jolt when he slid his rough, callused palm against her soft, much smaller one. "You always drive while thinking too much, Kat?"

"Katherine."

"Yeah…Kat suits you better than Katherine."

"Hmm." She considered that. "I guess, since you've seen me at my worst, not to mention heard my most embarrassing ramblings yesterday… Katherine does seem awfully formal." She smiled. "And you're not annoying. Just…" She lifted a shoulder. "Mysterious."

Well, at least she hadn't said a knuckle-dragging Neanderthal, which was what date number two had called him last night when he'd commented that her caviar tasted like fish bait. *That* date hadn't made it past dessert.

"Since you won't let me pay you," she suggested, "at least let me get you a soda."

"Sold," he said against his better judgment. But her eyes grabbed him, and he didn't know why.

"And all you have to do in return…" She led him down the hall again, past a large dining area to the kitchen, where she smiled at him, the one that made him a little dizzy. "Is tell me about yourself."

"There's not much to say." He accepted the can of soda.

"I doubt that." She grabbed another for herself. "Here, let me help you. Where are you from? What do you do?"

Steve had told him just that morning he needed to make more of an effort to open up. If he didn't, a woman was never going to trust him, and without trust, he wouldn't get what he'd come for.

Well, he wasn't getting it anyway, but suddenly he couldn't come up with a reason to rush off into the night. "I'm from Alaska. I'm a bush pilot."

"So what's a bush pilot from Alaska doing in Seattle?"

Yeah, good question. He had an answer, he just wasn't sure she really wanted to hear it, but Nick didn't have a lot of experience with hedging or lying. He spoke in truths, always, even when people didn't want to hear it. *Open up,* Steve had said, mostly because he'd been the one to set Nick up on the two failed dates.

Open up. Okay, here goes. "I'm in town to get a wife."

KATHERINE HAD just taken a sip of her soda when Nick spoke those words, and it definitely went down the wrong pipe. Coughing, eyes watering, throat burning, hand to her chest, she wheezed for a long moment. A wife?

He was here for a *wife?*

Nick started toward her, clearly concerned, but when Katherine lifted a hand, signaling she was all right, he relaxed back against the counter.

That was good, because she couldn't think when he got so close.

And no, unfortunately, she couldn't blame that on being afraid of him, or even being nervous. Maybe she had been both of those things around him—for about ten seconds.

But now she just felt…aware. *Extremely* aware. "You probably should have waited until I'd put the drink down to make a joke like that," she said, and smiled.

He didn't. "I wasn't joking."

"Right. You're here to get a…" Her eyes widened when he simply nodded. "Wife," she finished weakly. "What, is there a store where women line up, waiting to be purchased?"

"Yeah, Steve's store."

When she just stared at him, he rubbed the back of his neck. "A good friend of mine set up a meeting with several different women. All of them said they'd marry me and come back to Alaska to help take care of my kids." He reached for the soda he'd put down on the counter and took another sip. Over the can, his dark eyes lit with both frustration and good humor. "Turns out they hate Alaska, hate pilots and really hate kids." He shoved his fingers through his hair again, and she felt the tension grow within him. "Not a good match."

"You're really looking for a wife."

"Yes." The humor in his dark eyes faded, replaced by an intensity she couldn't look away from. "My kids mean everything to me. I need a mother for them, desperately, but I won't bring them any more pain by getting the wrong one."

"The wrong… *Wait*." She straightened, moved a little closer. His gaze never wavered. "You're serious."

"I am." He reached into his back pocket and pulled out his wallet. From inside he removed a small picture and handed it to her. "Here's my kids. Leila, the Tlingit lady who's been caring for them, can't keep up anymore. There aren't any other women in the area. I'd hire someone but I've gone that route before. Baby-sitters don't love and cherish and care for them the way I want them to be loved and cherished and cared for. Look, you want your own kid badly enough to consider going to a sperm bank. I've got three ready-made.''

She stared at him in shock. ''That's different.''

''How?''

Yeah, *how?* Lightly she ran her finger over the picture of the little girls, three beautiful little girls.

''That's Annie,'' he said, pointing to the oldest. ''She's four. And Emily, she's two, and then there's Kayla, the baby at ten months.''

They were all smiling—Annie with careful precision, Emily with pure mischief and Kayla with her fist in her mouth.

Katherine's heart melted. ''Don't you have any family to help you?''

His eyes were bleak before he shuttered them from her. ''None.''

''But…what happened to their mother?''

''She died in childbirth with Kayla.''

If she'd thought her heart had melted before… ''But, Nick, you can't just shop for a wife the way you would…a *car.*''

''Why not?''

''Why not?'' She laughed, then stopped abruptly when he didn't laugh back. ''Because there's got to be a friendship. A growth in that friendship to more…then a strong relationship…''

''It doesn't have to go that way.''

Was he that dense, or just desperate? She looked

at him and decided he was neither, just very, very honest. And waiting for her reaction.

"I need a wife, Kat."

"It sounds like you need a baby-sitter."

"I told you, I want more for my girls than that. I need a *wife*. You'd be perfect."

When his words sank in, she gawked at him. "There's quite a bit wrong with that statement. Where do you want me to start?"

"With 'I do.'"

She laughed. "This is the twenty-first century. Single people raise kids all the time. My mother did it from the time I was nine."

"What happened to your father?"

"He...went away."

"Ah." He winced. "He left you. I'm sorry."

"No. He didn't leave us like that—he didn't go on purpose. He...went to prison, actually." She crossed her arms. "We're talking about single parenting."

"No, you were talking about you."

She let out a soft breath. How to explain that she'd waited her entire life for hearts-and-flowers, dream-come-true love? And that a tiny part of her had started to worry they didn't exist? But even so, she desperately wanted to hold out for such things. "How about a nanny?"

"A nanny has her own life. I want my kids to be someone's life. You're maternal. You'd be perfect."

"I look...*maternal?*" Ridiculously, she homed in on what he'd thought was such a compliment.

Would it be so hard for a man to consider her unbearably sexy for once? "Do you understand that's not exactly what a woman wants to hear?"

He blinked. "Why not? It's true. You're sweet, warm. I saw you with that kid. You didn't care he wasn't yours, you still had your heart in what you were doing."

"Well, of course I did. That's my job."

"No, Kat."

God, the way he said her name. "Katherine," she whispered. "I think we should stick with Katherine."

"Katherine's too cold. You're not cold, not anywhere close. And it's more than just your job. You sincerely cared about that kid. That's rare. And it's exactly what I need."

"You...think I'm rare?"

"I know it," he said very softly. "You're different. I like it, Kat."

The man was crazy. She was crazy. And yet... She looked down into his three little girls' innocent, smiling faces. "They're so young."

"I know. They need a mom." A muscle in his jaw ticked, and he sighed. "I want to give them a mom."

"Oh, Nick." Her heart constricted hard at his situation. He was not as rough and tumble as she'd thought. Yes, he was a guy through and through, and big and rough around the edges. But the way he loved his daughters... He was desperate to help them, and she imagined a man like Nick Spencer didn't deal well with being desperate. "I'm so sorry about losing their mother. To lose a soul mate—"

"Cassandra was a close friend, the mother of my children. A great woman. But she wasn't my soul mate."

"But... I don't understand. A marriage...that's the union of two people in love, two people who can't stand to be apart. Two soul mates."

"Not this time." He sighed. "Cassandra...she had a hard life, an impossible childhood. We... bonded on that, I guess. But she didn't believe in love, not between a man and a woman. All she wanted from me was children and a home of her own."

"That's...sad," she breathed. "Sad for you. Did she break your heart?"

"Just looking at her broke my heart. But that was pity and friendship, not love. In hindsight anyway. The match between us was...a comfortable one, a necessary one."

Her mouth fell open. "What about love? Romance?"

"What about them?"

"Don't you want them in your life?"

"No. Why would I?"

"Um...because they're wonderful?"

He shook his head. "Look, it didn't work out for me the first time, and now I don't have the time for such things."

This was beyond her realm of understanding. Even with the problems her parents had faced, they'd loved each other. They'd loved their children. Katherine had never doubted that. She didn't know Nick at all, but looking into his tanned, rugged face, into his dark eyes waiting for her to explain why he needed love, she understood he must have had one of those childhoods lacking in love not to have any clue as to what he was missing. It made her sad for him, and she wanted to know more.

"You've experienced this love thing?" he asked her. "To give you such knowledge?"

"My family loves me. My friends love me—"

"We're talking about between a man and a woman, Kat. You've experienced that?"

"Okay...no," she admitted. She'd had a few boyfriends. One in high school, whom she hadn't slept with, two in college, both of whom she had slept with and then a brief but wild fling right after college. Lust, yes. Love...definitely not. "Not exactly."

"So you don't know."

"Not firsthand," she admitted.

His gaze flared with triumph. "Uh-huh."

"Look, just because I haven't experienced love

doesn't mean anything. I still believe in it. I believe it exists out there—'' Just look at her dreams. ''And if you're patient, you can find it.''

''Patient?'' He spread his hands, studied his work-roughened palms. ''I don't think so. I don't know about love, finding it or otherwise. What I *do* know is I need a wife. And I will find one.''

''Just like that.''

''Just like that.''

She stared at him, and he stared right back. For him, it really was that simple and straightforward. ''You really think you'll find a woman who'll happily go back with you and tend to the needs of your family in return for room and board?''

''And a decent life. More than decent. I make a good living and have a nice house. You wouldn't want for anything.''

Oh my God. He was utterly, one hundred percent serious about this.

''Think of it as a partnership,'' he said with a shrug. ''My first marriage was a great partnership.''

''But…'' Color tinged her cheeks at the thought, but she had to say it, had to know. ''What about your *personal* needs?''

''I'll share the cooking. And I clean up after myself. I don't require any attention.''

''I'm talking about…*sexually*.'' She whispered the last word, and expected him to laugh.

He didn't. But an odd light did come into his

eyes, an almost tender one, if she could believe he had tenderness in him. "I've never had a problem getting a woman in my bed," he said a little gruffly. "I wouldn't go looking for that where I wasn't welcome."

Oh my. She had the feeling that with this man, just about anything would be welcome. "I have to lock up now," she told him.

"Of course." He put the picture of his children away, but not without one last long look, his thumb running lightly over them.

"You miss them," she said.

"Yes."

That didn't surprise her. It was clear how much he loved them, and the extent he'd go to in order to see them cared for.

But it was barbaric.

So why, then, was she so drawn to this big man and the picture of his family? "Again, I'm so sorry about yesterday. I hope you find what you're looking for," she said softly, feeling all sorts of reactions leaping inside her at his proximity.

He looked down into her face. "I will."

Katherine watched him go, the oddest yearning spreading deep within her, warming her. It was similar to the yearning that had nearly driven her to keep her appointment at the sperm bank.

Only stronger, much stronger.

She just needed to get home. Needed to hug Carlos. Needed rest, and maybe chocolate first, lots of it.

But she couldn't get the big, gruff, rough and tumble man out of her head.

*I hope you find what you're looking for,* she'd told him, and she might have been talking to herself. "I hope I find what I'm looking for, too," she whispered into the night, and shut and locked the door.

Her cell phone was ringing, and it turned out to be her mother.

"Tell me you didn't go get yourself a baby the way Drew seems to think you did," Helen Kinard said.

Katherine sighed. "Drew has a big mouth."

"Of course he does. I taught him everything he knows."

"Mom—"

"My goodness, Katherine, a sperm bank?"

"Yes, but—"

"The whole thing just sounds so..." Her mother's voice trailed off, horrified.

"Simple?"

"I was going to say *complicated,* Katherine. It's all very complicated. You can't just go—" she lowered her voice to a whisper "—get inseminated."

"Sure you can, you just—"

"You know what I mean. Honey, you need a husband to raise kids."

*You didn't.* Katherine swallowed the cruel retort.

Hurting her mother, her sweet, kind, long-suffering mother, was not on her to-do list. "Mom, I didn't keep the appointment. I'm not going to go."

"Good. Please, honey, I know you don't necessarily believe this, but true love is the only way to have a child."

True love. Yes, that's what she wanted, with all her heart.

It just didn't seem to want her back.

## CHAPTER FOUR

"SO WHAT ARE YOU GOING TO DO?" Steve asked as he shoved a good third of his burger into his mouth. He had two more on the plate in front of him.

Nick sighed and stared at his own untouched food. "I don't know."

"You could, you know, buy a wife on the Internet." Steve chewed for a moment. "Well, probably."

"I'm not that desperate."

"Yes, you are. You're in need, buddy." He reached for another burger. "Three little girls under the age of five? Holy shit, you're in need all right. Big time."

Nick sighed and pushed around his French fries. "Yeah."

"You know, while I was sitting here waiting for you, I was doing the math. In a few years you're going to have three teenagers. Three *girl* teenagers." Steve grinned. "You remember girl teenagers."

Nick was trying not to.

"So whatcha going to do when the doorbell rings,

and standing there is a replica of you as a teenage boy, wanting to ask Annie out? And you know damn well what the kid is thinking, because we thought it, too.''

''Are you trying to help here? Because you're not.''

''You should consider buying stock in things like Tampax.'' Unbelievably, he continued to shovel in food. ''And you remember how moody they are? Better buy stock in Midol, too. Do they make Junior Midol?''

Appetite gone, Nick shoved his plate away.

Steve's smile faded. ''Maybe we should just concentrate on the immediate worry. Finding you a woman. I mean, if you do it right, the teenage years won't be so bad. Maybe.''

''Right.'' He hated to need anything. But as he knew all too well, sometimes life sucked. ''Maybe I should just forget it. Just get into my plane and fly home.''

''Sure. Back to your own personal hell.''

Personal hell or not, under any other circumstances he would go back. He wanted, needed to get home to be with the kids. To get back to normal, or as normal as he could make it for them.

But he lived outside Anchorage, way out. There was no Forrester Square Day Care. There was… nothing. If he was going to work, which he had to, he needed someone to help him, someone to love the girls, someone to share the overwhelming everyday responsibilities of raising them so he could financially support them.

It wasn't as if he was in the poorhouse, but he'd grown up that way. He'd been shuffled from foster home to foster home in Anchorage, with nothing of his own until he'd gone into middle school and started working at a small, private airport for cash—doing whatever the owner, Paddy McQuintle, had needed, including mopping up oil spills and carrying coffee to rich clients.

It had been through Paddy that Nick had gotten his love of flying, and his first plane. And it was Paddy who'd taught him how to rebuild that clunker and then sell it for a big enough profit to buy another.

He'd paid Paddy off years ago, and in fact was on his fourth plane at the moment, but he still had a soft spot for the old man he'd do anything for.

And when the right woman came along, he'd willingly give her everything as well, whatever she needed—sex, no sex, money, *anything*—if only in return she could love his children.

Was that so much to ask?

Apparently, yes.

A feeling of helplessness overwhelmed him, a man who never allowed anything in life to overwhelm him.

He'd been through some tough times before. Being orphaned was tough, and so were the ensuing foster homes. School had been tough, too, without anyone really caring how he did. But then Paddy had come along, bullying him to get good grades or he wouldn't be allowed to work on the planes.

A fate worse than death.

Still, even with Paddy's support, it had been rough getting his business going. *Keeping* it going. Buying what he needed in parts and fuel…

But *this*. This spot he was in now beat anything he'd ever faced.

For the first time in his life, Nick had no idea what he was going to do. He didn't have the kind of job he could drag three little girls to. Being in the air all day was no kind of life for them.

And yet if he couldn't do his job, he couldn't feed them.

Being alone was his style. Without a family and a lot of ties, it had been easy. But now, what he would give for a single family tie.

Not going to happen. His mother had died when he was two, and since she'd never named his father, there'd been no one to claim shared blood with, or at least not that he knew about.

The only connection he had to his past was Paddy, and of course the man sitting across from him wolfing down burgers as if they were going out of style. He and Steve had been in a foster home together in high school, and back then they'd pretended they were brothers.

Now they just acted like it.

Steve would do anything for Nick. Nick knew that, but as a carpenter in Seattle, where he'd settled after barely graduating high school, there wasn't much Steve could offer.

They were out of available women.

"What about putting out an ad?" Steve asked now, chasing his burgers with a beer.

"No way," Nick said firmly. Yeah, he wanted a wife, but not sight unseen. And it wasn't the "look" of a woman he worried about, either.

"Well, then." Steve shrugged. "You're done in."

Nick's thoughts drifted to Kat, as they had more than once tonight. The day before, alone in her half-darkened day care, he'd had the crazy thought that *she* could be the one.

And he still thought so, actually. If only he could convince her. He tossed some bills down on the table and stood up.

"Where you going?" Steve eyed Nick's French fries. "Hey, you going to eat those?"

Nick pushed his plate closer to Steve. "They're yours. I'll call you later."

Steve opened a bottle of ketchup and dumped it on the fries. "You're going back to see her again, aren't you."

"Her who?"

"Her who intrigued you last night. The woman with the lead foot." Steve dug into the fries with gusto. "Be careful with that one."

"She's just a woman."

Steve nodded. "Sure. But there's something different about her."

"What do you mean, different?"

"I mean…" Steve lifted his gaze and Nick was surprised to see worry there. "You're thinking about her, you're restless about her. And it's not just because she's tall and curvy and pretty. You never really cared about looks." He licked his fingers. "You're going back for seconds."

"There was never a first," Nick said with an attempt at humor he didn't quite feel.

"Yes, but you've never gone back before. *Never,*" Steve repeated softly.

Nick shrugged. "Maybe I think she has wife potential."

"Sure. And she does. It's just that with this whole needing-a-wife thing…well, up until now, it's never been about you. It's been about the girls, you know?"

"Yeah. So?"

"So with this chick, it's about her. And you." Steve looked at him. "It's about your first marriage, and much as I cared about Cassandra, it's about

what she could never give you. And I think you
know it.''

"I don't even know Kat.''

"But you want to. You want to know more than
if she can love your kids. Am I right?''

Hell. Yeah, he was right, and no, Nick didn't really understand it. "I've got to go.''

"I know. Good luck, buddy.''

Nick nodded and walked out into the Seattle
night. It was chilly, and wet, but he didn't mind,
either. He stuck his hands into his pockets and
started walking. Being only a few blocks from the
day-care center, he'd just stop by. Just to see if this
inexplicable interest was as two-sided as he suspected.

Around him, people were bundled up in the late
spring night. A lady passed him in a long wool coat,
her scarf wrapped around her face as if a blizzard
were blowing. A man had his hood up and his arms
crossed in front of him, hunched against the breeze.

Nick smiled. Used to far harsher weather, he
walked down the street in a simple chambray shirt
and jeans, perfectly fine. The area was fancy, with
expensive homes mingled in with equally expensive
businesses.

He passed Caffeine Hy's, the coffee shop where
he'd first seen Kat. It was the fourth coffee shop
he'd passed, which made him shake his head in

wonder. This whole city just seemed so decadent, so…huge.

At last he came to stand beneath the banner proclaiming Forrester Square Day Care.

There was a light burning inside. He checked his watch. Five forty-five. No doubt, given how he knew Kat felt about this place, she'd still be there.

He'd probably have more luck winning the lottery than convincing her to come to Alaska and be his wife. Hell, he'd probably have more luck waving a big sign right here in the street that read Wanted: Wife!

But Nick didn't play the lottery, and making a fool of himself had never appealed. Bottom line, something was telling him he had to go for this, he had to try.

Even before he opened the door he heard raised voices. Adult voices, one female, one male, both shrill and angry.

A third voice joined in, a soft, warm voice trying to calm and soothe.

Kat.

Suddenly he was very glad he'd come.

KATHERINE WOULD have said she enjoyed all the parents she met through the day care. It was important to her and her staff to have a good rapport with everyone, and even more important that there be a mutual respect. In the case of divorce or separation, the staff had always been able to maintain an easy atmosphere with both parents, and prided themselves in that.

But the parents of one sweet four-year-old, Sabrina Molina, were bitterly divorced. For the most part, Sabrina lived with her mother, Cissy, a sweet, hardworking woman Katherine was quite fond of.

Once in a while, however, Sabrina visited her father, Marco Molina, and whenever he brought Sabrina in for the day, there were always issues. He would forget to pack her a lunch, or hadn't bothered to dress her. Often he didn't pick her up on time, and if he did, it was with a disinterest that worried Katherine. She felt relieved whenever she knew Sabrina was going home with Cissy.

Today, due to a lack of communication, both Cissy and Marco had come for the child.

Worse, everyone else had left for the day, leaving Katherine alone to deal with the heated tempers. She'd given Marco and Cissy a moment alone to discuss the problem while she occupied Sabrina with her favorite book, but she could hear the gradually rising voices and knew it was all going downhill.

She hoped they'd resolve the problem themselves, without any interference from her. Whenever anyone tried to get involved, it never failed to infuriate Marco.

''If you give a mouse a cookie,'' she read to Sabrina, increasing her volume as Marco started yelling.

Cissy yelled right back. "It *is* my day—just look at a calendar! You have this coming weekend, remember? You wouldn't trade with me when I asked!"

"Because you always want to trade! You don't ever want me to have her!"

"Because you don't take good enough care of her!"

Katherine glanced uneasily over her shoulder at the ruckus. Cissy and Marco were nose to nose now, and Marco's hands curled into fists at his side.

Oh boy. Not good. "Sabrina," she said quietly, closing the book. Neither of them wanted to hear if the mouse needed milk to go with his cookie, not at the moment, and there was no sense pretending. "Why don't you go get a brownie off the tray in the kitchen?"

Sabrina's eyes were huge. "Are you going to give them a time-out for yelling in the Events Room?"

"You know what? Make that *two* brownies. Go on now, sweetie." Katherine smiled and ruffled Sabrina's hair.

Waiting until the little girl was gone, she stepped between the two fighting parents.

"I have the schedule," she said as the front door of the school opened and closed behind her. She heard footsteps move down the hall and stop in the doorway, but she didn't dare take her eyes off Marco. He was a lit rocket now, one she needed to defuse. "There's no reason to do this, not with your child within hearing distance."

Marco's furious gaze sliced from his ex-wife to Katherine. "Don't tell me what to do."

"I just don't want any trouble here," she said calmly, even though her heart was beating a rather unsteady tattoo against her ribs. "I don't think you want any trouble, either."

"Don't tell me what I want."

"Marco, you know your day is tomorrow," Cissy broke in. "Please, don't make a scene, don't upset Sabrina. Just come back tomorrow. You can have her tomorrow."

Marco didn't back down an inch. His rage poured off him in waves, tumbling over Katherine, who stood between him and the object of that rage. She held her breath and waited for him to make a decision.

"Kat," said another male voice from right behind them. "Are you all right?"

Katherine knew that low, husky timbre. In only a few days it had become almost unbearably familiar. In fact—not a big surprise—she'd dreamed of it. Of him.

She hadn't expected to ever hear it again, though.

Nick's boots hit the floor with each loose-hipped step as he came to a stop right at her side. He wore his usual jeans today, and a dark blue, long-sleeved shirt streaked with a few raindrops. Like a native Seattleite, he didn't appear to have bothered with an umbrella. That was all Katherine could catch of him out of her peripheral vision because she hadn't taken her eyes off Marco and didn't intend to.

Nick settled a protective hand at the small of her back.

Or was that possessive?

Standing so close to her that his chest bumped into her arm, he looked down into her face with such authority that she found herself utterly compelled to look right back at him.

"What's going on?" he asked.

"I, um…" Nerves had her voice quivering, giving her away. "I have one child left in my care." She cleared her throat. "And…both her mother and father showed up at the same time."

"Hmm." Nick moved his hand slightly, just a quick up and down gesture, which she found incredibly calming. Who'd have thought the man, big and gruff as he was, would be able to do that for her? "There was some mix-up about who was to pick her up. But that's cleared up now. Right, Mr. Molina?"

Marco turned his head and eyed Nick, who with his impressive height and bulk was not someone Katherine would want to mess with.

Apparently Marco felt the same way. With a look

of distaste, he slowly backed away, then stormed out the front door of the building.

"Well." Cissy smiled, but the attempt was strained. "Thank you." She glanced at Nick, who hadn't budged, who in fact still had his hand on Katherine. "Thank you both. I'll just grab Sabrina and be on my way."

Katherine waited, but even after Cissy and Sabrina had gone, Nick didn't move. Nor did he take his hand off her back. Any other man she knew would have backed up to give her some space, but not Nick. He just stayed right next to her. She could feel the warmth of him, the sheer strength, seeping into her. His fingers were spread wide, another difference between him and any other man. Even as she thought about it, his thumb made a slow, sweeping pass over as much of her as he could reach.

That should have seemed too forward. After all, he was a perfect stranger, or close enough. But somehow she just knew it was a Nick thing, a one hundred percent guy response to their proximity.

And she had no doubt, Nick Spencer was one hundred percent guy.

Just thinking it made her knees a little wobbly. If he'd wanted to make her aware of him, he'd done it. If he'd wanted to make sure she knew he was right there, he'd done that, too.

He'd set her on fire with one touch.

"Does that happen often?" he asked, the low

rumble of his voice close enough to her ear that it sent a shiver—the good kind—down her back.

"No, thankfully." She let out the breath she'd been holding.

"He wasn't going to back down."

"No. But then you showed up."

He stared at her, then let out a frustrated breath. "That worries me."

"I can take care of myself, Nick. I always have."

He lifted his other hand, and with a light touch for such a big man, stroked a finger over her cheek, tucking a wayward strand of hair behind her ear.

The pad of his finger was rough, and she liked it. Yet another shiver raced down her spine.

Impossibly, his eyes darkened even more, heating as they did.

Good Lord, what was he thinking to make him look at her like that?

"You're tougher than you look," he murmured.

Since she didn't quite trust her voice, she nodded. He let out a rough laugh, shocking her. It was the first she'd heard from him and she supposed she shouldn't thrill to the sound, but she did. She liked the sound of his humor, and also liked the look of it in his eyes. "I *am* tougher than I seem."

"I like that about you," he said softly. "Damn, but I really do."

"I'm glad you approve." She meant to say this

dryly, just a little sarcastically, but it came out rather breathless, which made her wince.

His mouth actually curved. "Regardless of your toughness factor, I'm glad I showed up when I did."

"I'm glad you did, too. But not to be rude, *why* did you?"

"I wanted to know if you'd thought about my proposal."

She blinked. "Proposal?"

"The one where you come to Alaska with me."

"The one where I—" She shook her head and let out a little amazed laugh. The man was a complete throwback. No matter how mind-boggling sexy he was, he didn't have a clue. "You never really said—"

"No? Then I'm saying it now." He straightened and looked her directly in the eyes, his own dark and serious and intent. "Come with me to Alaska."

"To raise your kids."

"To raise my kids."

"To be your wife."

"To be my wife."

She swallowed hard. "Give up everything in my life, just like that, to be with a man I know nothing about."

He frowned. "I'm an open book."

She looked into his baffled face and laughed again.

"Okay." He grimaced. "So I'm not quite an open book. What do you want to know? Just ask."

"Um…"

"I already told you I can cook and clean up after myself. I work hard and can provide for you. What else could you possibly need?"

Right. What else? Nothing really… Except for love. "Obviously we don't have the same needs in a spouse," she said. "I'm looking for a soul mate. Not a roommate."

"Soul mate." On his tongue, the words sounded foreign.

"We talked about love, romance," she reminded him. "But are you telling me you don't believe in soul mates, either?"

"No."

No thinking about it, no hedging. Just no. What had his life been like to make him so hard? He was willing to marry her, practically sight unseen, simply because she was warm and good with kids. He was willing to take care of her and provide for her. No quibble or qualm.

And he asked for so little in return, just the care of his daughters.

But what about him? Had no one ever been there for him? She couldn't believe it, and for some reason, maybe because of her save-the-world heart, she wanted to know more. Accepting that she was crazy, she said, "How about we start with a casual date out?"

"What?"

"A date."

"A date," he repeated slowly.

"Yes, you know, where you pick me up, we eat together, maybe dance, then say 'good night.' Not 'I do.'"

"Oh."

She had to laugh at his confusion. He hadn't asked her out, he'd only asked her to marry him.

"You want to…date me."

Smiling, she nodded.

"And *then* you'll come to Alaska with me?"

Her heart kicked hard. "My entire life is here," she said gently. "My friends, my work." And it was a good life. "And yet…"

He pounced on that. "And yet…?"

"And yet…I'd go to the ends of the earth for love," she whispered.

He just stared at her. "You're right. Let's start with a date."

## CHAPTER FIVE

KATHERINE STARED up at him. "Now?" she asked.

"Yep."

"You want to go on a date *right now?*"

No, what Nick wanted to do *right now* was to take her home. That he also wanted to toss her into his bed didn't count. This was about his kids, not him.

But with Kat, the interesting, versatile, warm yet tough, inexplicable Kat, he couldn't move at warp speed like he wanted. She needed a different pace, and oddly enough, he found he had the patience to give her that pace.

If she hurried.

"Nick?"

He looked down into her face and felt the tug of attraction. It wasn't purely physical, though there was plenty of that. She was tall, willowy, with hints of curves that made his hands itch to explore.

And yet…there was more, much more. He wanted to know about her, what made her smile and laugh. What she thought about basketball, and fishing, and life in general. Did she like to fly? Did she like the cold? Did she like to have wild animal sex to keep warm—

Okay, he was back to the physical wanting. Maybe that was good, where his comfort level lay. Surface feelings only. He'd been doing that for so long it startled him to realize he was thinking about more. "Yeah, let's go out right now." A *date,* complete with awkward pauses and obligatory conversation and more awkward pauses. Why did women value dates so much, anyway? In his mind they were a ridiculous waste of time.

She was perfect for what he needed, he knew that already.

But he supposed she had to come to the same conclusion. Damn it. "Dinner."

She looked at him for a long moment, clearly assessing him for mental instability, murderous tendencies or malintent.

"Kat?"

"Dinner is good, in a crowded place, of course. Carlos is with a friend today so I'm free."

"Carlos…" All sorts of possibilities rushed through his head. Husband. Lover—

"My foster child."

"Oh." Relief filled him. Until he realized she could still have that husband or lover. "You're not—"

"Married?" She laughed. "Heck of a time to ask

now, don't you think? Considering you've already asked me to marry you?''

"Kat—"

"I'm not married, Nick. You can take that panicked look off your face. If I was married or attached, I'd never have been attracted to you. Nor would I have been contemplating a sperm bank.''

"You're attracted to me." He couldn't help it, he grinned.

"From panic to smug." She shook her head. "You are such a guy, Nick Spencer. A guy all the way through.''

"God, I hope so.''

"Carlos is very much like you," she said with a helpless smile. "Completely male. He's just turned thirteen, complete with teenage attitude and lack of clothing sense, but beyond all that, he's got a heart of gold." She sighed. "I'm trying to adopt him.''

"That's…'' Amazing, he wanted to say. *She* was amazing. "That's really nice.''

"I know." She beamed at him, a smile from the heart that made him a little dizzy. "So…dinner?''

"Yes." They'd start there, with burgers or whatever, and see—

"A friend of mine just opened a new restaurant in Pike Place Market, which isn't far. I've been meaning to go check it out, but Carlos isn't into anything but burgers and fries.''

He and Carlos were even more alike than she

knew. He resigned himself to froufrou food at a little place where his knees would bang into the table and there'd be no elbow room. He hated restaurants like that, where he left hungry because the portions were too small or the food just plain stupid. "It's probably too late to get reservations," he said far too hopefully.

"I could call…" And she was off.

The woman made his head spin. He watched her move out of the room, presumably to use the phone. She was a take-charge sort of person, and somehow he'd imagined bringing a woman home who was more content to let *him* run the show, a woman who'd let him make the decisions.

He couldn't imagine Kat letting anyone decide anything for her.

Before he could accept that he was crazy and run out the door, she was back with a smile. "It's no problem, we're in."

*Perfect.*

"You ready?"

Yes, he was quite ready. To be hungry. But at least he could spend the time proving to her he was a polite, well-rounded citizen with some manners. Husband material. They went in his Jeep, with Kat giving him directions delivered with a smile, making his head swim when she leaned in to point something out to him about her city.

The night was a wet one. Big surprise. Rain

slashed at the windows. The lights and the cars around them shimmered and weaved through the whirl of the windshield wipers racing back and forth, whisking away the rain. Next to him, Kat smelled like something soft and edible, and she smiled at him again when she caught him looking at her.

It all combined to create an intimacy in the confines of the vehicle, an anticipation he couldn't attribute as purely sexual.

God, she smelled good, sort of like a wildflower he couldn't quite place. Had Cassandra smelled good? It bugged him that he couldn't remember.

His head was spinning.

Or still spinning. It had been since he'd met her.

They came into Pike Place Market, which was a six-block area of shops and restaurants and various stalls assembled like some sort of farmers' market, with vendors peddling their wares, everything from fresh vegetables to fish to flowers.

They pulled up to an awning in front of a corner restaurant. A man with an umbrella ran out and opened the driver's door. "Good evening, sir."

Before Nick could say a word, he was ushered out of the car and handed a ticket.

"Valet," the attendant said, and though he looked to be about twelve, he slid into the driver's seat.

Nick looked down at his valet ticket. Some teenage kid was going to park his car. Since it was a rental, he decided to deal with it. With a sigh, he went around to get Kat, but she'd already been escorted up the three steps to the door of the restaurant, which was being held open by yet another smiling attendant who looked even younger.

People smiled a lot in this damn city.

He followed her up the steps and inside. Before he could take a breath, the hostess was helping Kat off with her jacket and taking that away, too.

So much for showing any charm or manners. He hadn't had a chance to. The restaurant was laid out like an old theater, with everything from hanging lights and cameras to curtains and old stage props. The servers were dressed in black trousers and white button-down shirts with suspenders, and appeared to be singing old show tunes as they walked around with their trays filled with exotic-looking food.

No burgers in sight.

"Look." Kat pointed off to the left, to a candlelit stage where a man was playing a piano, accompanying the servers. She sighed with pleasure. "Isn't this wonderful? They wrote the place up in the paper last week and I've been dying to come see."

What was "wonderful" was her smile, her excitement as she craned her neck to catch every last detail.

"I can't wait to see how good the food tastes here," she said.

To Nick, food was a necessity, fuel for his body.

Hell, half the time he was lucky to shove a sandwich down his throat by midday, and dinner with three little wild ones was always a harried, eat-your-peas-don't-throw-them affair that left him exhausted.

The hostess promised to tell the chef, Kat's friend, that they were here, and led them into one of the main dining rooms.

Nick walked behind Katherine, his eyes automatically running down the length of her body. The knit material of her dress slid over her slim spine and rounded hips, clinging with every step.

*Baby-sitter,* he repeated to himself. *Caregiver.* This was what he needed her for.

Not her mouthwatering body.

"Doesn't it smell good in here?" She craned her neck back to whisper at him, and caught him ogling her.

"Here you go," the hostess said before he could respond. She gestured Kat to the first chair, then took what seemed like an excessive amount of time handing him his menu. She made a big deal out of setting his napkin in his lap—Christ, he could put his own napkin in his lap—then reciting the specials for the evening.

When she finally moved away, Kat leaned across the table. "You were staring at my...tush."

"I know." God help him, she called the finest ass ever seen by man a *tush*. "It's just that it's a very nice tush, Kat."

She just stared at him.

He really needed to stop trying to talk to women, period. "I'm sorry. I—"

"You're a very different sort of man," she said. "I mean, you're…"

He winced and waited.

"Forthright." She laughed a little and shook her head. "And that's an understatement. From what I know of you, and it isn't much, you're bluntly honest and have no trouble just saying whatever it is you want to."

Here came the blow off. "Yeah, but—"

"I like it," she whispered, and smiled.

And damn if his heart didn't tip on its side.

"Good evening, folks." This from yet another waiter. Or attendant. Or whatever the hell he was. He was tall, thin, sporting a ridiculously curled mustache, and had a towel folded over his hands. "Would you care for a drink this evening? We have a fab wine list."

Nick would rather have a beer. He needed it to quench his odd thirst, though he doubted any liquid was going to do that.

"I'll have an iced tea, please." Kat looked at Nick. "I'm not a big drinker." She shot him a self-deprecatory grin. "I shouldn't say this, but alcohol makes me a cheap date."

*Wine, please.* "I'll just have an iced tea, too," he said, and was rewarded by Kat with a smile he was sure anyone else would have said was sweet, but he was still on the cheap-date thing and found everything unbearably sexy at the moment.

He had no idea what she expected to get out of this evening, but he'd be content just to look at her. Her face was so expressive, so utterly captivating, he found it difficult to take his eyes off her.

That problem was cut short when the chef came out and talked to them for so long, Nick began to wonder if she'd ever shut up, and also, who the hell was cooking in her absence?

When she finally left, and Nick could relax again, a tray appeared, a "surprise special" just for them.

Sushi.

He hated sushi.

In disbelief he stared at the tray. His stomach growled, unhappily.

"Sushi," Kat said in a strange voice. "She was talking so fast, I didn't… Hmm. Well, there is a basil scent, I think, and I do like basil, but…"

He took his eyes off the towering platter of extremely funky-looking raw fish and looked at her. "But…?"

"I, um…" She bit her lower lip. Reddened.

He tried to think of what had happened. Had she burped and he'd missed it?

She eyed the platter, tortured her lower lip some more, then leaned forward. Oddly enough, his gaze caught on her sexy mouth and he missed what she said. "Pardon?"

"I said…" She looked around, then cupped her mouth so only he could hear her. "I hate sushi." She sat back. "I'm sorry, please don't let it ruin your evening, but—"

"Kat—"

"I know!" She covered her face. "It's un-American! But I just can't. It's slimy, it's smelly, it's—"

"Kat." He actually felt like laughing. "I hate sushi, too."

Her jaw dropped.

And for the first time in a very long time, he felt a genuine smile split his face. "What do you say we drink our tea, then blow this Popsicle stand? Find a burger joint or something. With, please God, lots of fries. Tell me you love burgers and fries."

"I love burgers and fries."

"Great. Will you marry me?"

She stared at him, then laughed, then clapped her hands over her mouth. "I shouldn't laugh, because you're totally serious."

"Yeah. So what's the problem?"

"Nick…"

"Yes, Kat?"

At his mock docile expression and tone, she grinned. "You know I'm not going to up and move to Alaska just because you asked."

"Right. We're going to date until I talk you into it." He tossed some money down on the table while she explained and apologized to her friend. Then he reached for her hand. "Let's go."

In the Jeep, she said, "I still can't believe you expect me to agree to marry you after just one date."

"How many dates do you anticipate it's going to take?"

"You're impossible," she said with a laugh.

AT THE BURGER JOINT she directed him to, they found a cozy booth in the corner. Nick slid in beside her rather than across from her, smiling innocently when she lifted a brow. "Too close?" he asked.

"It's close…" She shrugged and shot him a look he didn't dare decipher. "But not too close."

They ordered and then Kat turned her attention back to him. "Tell me about yourself. Other than you like to get your way and be in charge."

He grinned.

"Oh, is that not true?"

His brow rose. "You want me to admit I'm bull-headed, and sometimes an ass?"

"Well…" She laughed. "Yes."

He found himself laughing, too. "But you already know those things."

"*Talk,* Nick."

Man, the sound of his name on her lips… "Okay,

something about me. Well…'' He spread his hands.
''I like you.''

''That's very nice. But I want to hear about *you.*
You're a pilot.''

''Yep. I take people into the wilderness to fish,
hunt, whatever they need. I also deliver the mail and
supplies to several remote little towns and villages.''

''And you love it.''

''I love it,'' he agreed. ''Flying…there's a freedom there that's unimaginable until you do it. I
don't see myself giving it up until I'm too old to see
to land.''

She smiled. ''That'll probably be a while.''

''I'm hoping so.''

''And your girls…you said they're your only
family.''

''Yep.''

Her forearm was resting on the table, her fingers
wrapped around her water glass. Her nails were
short and unpolished, and she was wearing a brace-
let of shimmery, delicate beads. She shifted and covered his hand with hers. The touch electrified him,
and he turned his hand over to grasp her fingers in
his.

''What happened that you're all alone, Nick?''

He stared down at their hands, so different. Her
skin was creamy, smooth, her fingers long and ta-
pered. In comparison, his hand looked huge and
tanned. Tough.

Odd that, suddenly, he didn't feel tough.

"Nick?"

His smile faded some, he couldn't help it. "I lost my mother when I was two, and I never knew my dad. I spent most of my youth as a foster kid." He lifted a shoulder and tried to bring his smile back because she looked so sad for him. "It was actually better than it sounds, and look at me, I turned out okay."

She did look at him, slowly and thoroughly, her gaze running over his face, his chest and shoulders and arms—all she could see of him because of the table. "You did turn out pretty okay."

Her eyes had softened and so had her voice. Utterly captivated, he just looked at her. Not much had gone his way lately. But being with this woman, here, tonight, had become a pleasure he hadn't expected, and if the frantic pulse at the beat of her neck meant anything, or the way her lips had gently parted, her breath quickening, she felt the same.

He could think of one thing that he wanted to go his way.

He was going to kiss her. Right here, right now.

As if reading his mind, Kat dropped her gaze to his mouth, silently asking for the same thing.

Oh, yeah. He leaned in.

So did she.

The air crackled.

"Here's your food..." The waitress with the

lovely timing plopped the promised burgers and fries down in front of them and smacked her gum, grinning knowingly. "Enjoy."

Kat laughed and reached for a French fry. "I think she did that on purpose."

"She must not value her tips."

She laughed again, and the sound warmed Nick in a way few other things did. For a moment he could only look at her.

"What?" Kat shifted. "Do I have something in my teeth?"

He touched the corner of her mouth, where she did indeed have a smudge of ketchup. He sucked it off his finger.

At the sound, her breath shuddered out.

So did his.

"Nick—" A nervous little laugh escaped her. "Nick...you're moving so fast."

"I'm just sitting here."

"Yes, you're just sitting there. Thinking...*things*."

Uh-huh. Lots of things. Hot things. Sexual things. "I'm thinking it's nice, watching your pleasure in every little thing. Reading to a kid, the new decor of a restaurant...whatever. You enjoy it all. You're an interesting woman, Kat."

The waitress came back with refills of their drinks. When she left, Nick fed Kat another French fry, tempted to lean in and lick her lips with his, but he refrained. Barely. "That was a compliment, you know."

"I'm sure it was."

He laughed at her tone. "It was. What's the matter with being interesting, anyway?"

"Once in a while, maybe a woman wants to be more than interesting. Maybe she wants to be…oh, I don't know…unbearably sexy."

He nearly choked. "I can promise you," he said a little hoarsely, "you are unbearably sexy."

She stopped in the middle of lifting her drink to her mouth. Eyed him. Set her drink down. "I'm sorry. That came out like I was fishing for the compliment."

"Okay." He pushed their plates away, turned to face her and took her hands in his. "There's something else about me you should probably know. I never say anything I don't mean. I can promise you that."

"No promises." She shook her head. "I don't want promises from you. It's too soon."

"I don't have a lot of time."

"And I don't have anything but."

Right. With a frustrated breath, he downed his drink, then looked at her.

She burst out laughing.

"What?" He swiped at his mouth, wondering if he had ketchup all over it, too.

"Don't worry, you don't have anything on your face that I can lick off."

Damn.

"You're just so used to getting your own way," she said. "And when you don't, your irritation is all over your face for the world to see. You honestly don't get why I won't just drop everything and come with you?"

"Here you go," said their waitress, again appearing without a sound. "Your bill." With a pop of her gum and a wide wink, she sashayed away.

Kat took another look at him and grinned as she straightened. "Yep. Your every emotion…right across your face. Let's go before you do as you're thinking and kill her."

NICK WALKED Katherine to her door, a big warm hand low on her spine as he guided her up the steps. The night was dark, the air cool and breezy, with the occasional drop of rain falling down on them.

A large drop hit her arm and she was surprised it didn't steam. On every single first date she'd ever had, she'd felt too tall, too awkward, too…everything.

With Nick, there'd been no awkwardness. She felt alive. Cherished.

*Sexy.*

He was going to kiss her. He'd better kiss her.

They walked up the path to her front door and

stood beneath the porch light, surrounded by her colorful garden and the deep spring night. At the last step she turned and faced him. "That was fun. Even the sushi. Nick, I really appreciate—"

That was all she got out before he cupped her jaw in his hand, leaned in and covered her mouth with his. And ohmigod, his mouth. It was warm, firm and so delicious she melted....

HE PULLED BACK, slowly, so that their lips clung for an extra moment. The sucking sound they made when he finally straightened caused him to moan softly.

Her eyes fluttered open. "Nick..."

"There's something else I should tell you about me." His voice sounded a little raw, even to his own ears, but it was the best he could do after that kiss. "The way you say my name turns me on."

She opened her mouth, then closed it again, looking adorably confused and aroused.

Ah, hell, he was a goner. He kissed her again, and this time *she* moaned. With a shudder, Nick thrust deep inside her mouth.

She crowded closer, fisting the front of his shirt, then dancing her fingers upward, around his neck, as the two of them continued to explore and touch each other.

When he lifted his mouth from hers this time, her

eyes were sleepy-sexy, her mouth full and wet. He could only stare at her.

She stared right back, breathing as hard as he was, and looking like the tastiest treat he'd ever seen.

He was going to kiss her again, *had* to kiss her again. ''Kat—''

''Yes.'' She went up on tiptoe, and this time she made the move. When he opened his mouth, she dipped in, hesitant enough to make him ache, but brave enough to make the stand. He forced himself to be still, to let her set the pace, which she did when she pressed closer and ran her teeth over his tongue, making them both moan. Their mouths clung, and he tightened his grip on her, drawing in some serious air when she lifted her head.

''I don't suppose you're ready to come to Alaska?'' he managed to ask.

She was breathing funny, too, as if she'd just run a marathon. ''No.''

''Then I'll see you tomorrow.''

''Tomorrow?''

''And every day after that until I convince you.'' He kissed her jaw, his mouth gliding up to her ear, his tongue licking her once. Her helpless little whimper made his eyes cross with lust.

Damn, it had been a long time since he'd kissed like this. ''Night, Kat.''

''Night,'' she whispered, and fumbled with the door handle.

Good. He wasn't the only one turned into an idiot by what they'd just done. He smiled.

So did she, then she let herself inside and shut the door.

But even from the other side of that door, he could hear her sigh.

And his smile turned into a wide grin.

## CHAPTER SIX

THE NEXT MORNING Katherine stood in the kitchen, daydreaming out the window, when Carlos made his sleepy way in, brought there as usual by the scent of breakfast.

"Hey, sweetie." She took her mind off last night and smiled at him. "How are you doing?"

"Good." He looked her over while he yawned and scratched various body parts. "You're still grinning."

Katherine brought him a plate of eggs and toast, feeling a little burst of love just looking at him all rumpled and groggy. "Still grinning from what?"

"Your date." He rubbed his chest and yawned again, revealing a hint of the man he was going to become, and she found herself smiling at him.

She poured him some juice. "You know, before last night, I'd have said I had a better chance of getting hit by lightning than finding my Mr. Right...." She still felt that way, but at least the storm could possibly be in the neighborhood. She just needed a steel rod to hold.

Carlos merely nodded and continued to eat.

It was so utterly unlike him not to press for details, she frowned. "What's the matter?"

"Did you see yesterday's mail?" He nudged the stack in the middle of the table.

She flipped through the electric bill, the gas bill, the credit card bill... "Well, these look fun."

"The next one down."

It was an envelope from the department of children's services. More paperwork for the adoption. Just the other day the social worker had told her to expect it. She ripped open the envelope and flipped through the forms.

"It's okay," he whispered, and pushed back from the table. "You've changed your mind about me. It's no biggee. I understand—"

She grabbed his hand and halted his retreat. "Carlos..." Her voice caught. "No—"

"Honest, it's no problem."

"Do you remember when we talked about me adopting you?"

He swallowed hard. "Yeah."

"I've set the plan in motion. These are the forms I need to do that. That is...if *you're* still okay with it."

He just stared at her, and her heart cracked. "I'd love it if you were mine," she said. "I really would."

"Really?"

"Really." She tossed the forms aside and threw her arms around him. "What do you think?"

"Yes." He hugged her back, burying his face against her. "Yes."

IT WAS A work-from-home day for Katherine, which she tried to do every couple of weeks. Typically, she spent the first half of the morning cleaning her house, then the second half going over the accounting books for the day care.

By ten o'clock she was deep in cleaning mode. She wore raggedy old sweat bottoms and a tank top that had once, a very long time ago, been bright red. Now she couldn't even call it pink, the thing was so threadbare. But she was comfortable, and when it came to housework, it was all about comfort. She'd piled her hair on top of her head, wore yellow gloves that went up to her elbows, and was attacking the tile shower in her bathroom.

Although she had the radio tuned to her favorite talk show, her thoughts were a million miles away.

They were on last night.

She'd told Carlos about Nick on the way to school that morning. That he was from Alaska, and needed a wife for his girls.

She'd expected the kid to laugh at her.

Instead he'd cocked his head, studied her for a

long moment, then simply said, "Alaska would suit you."

"And how about you?" she'd asked, holding her breath for reasons that made no sense because she was not up and moving to Alaska. It was silly... "Would the place suit you, Carlos?"

"Are you kidding?" He'd smiled that slow, cocky smile that always made her want to smother him with love. "Fishing, mountains...bears. What could be cooler? And anyway..." He'd lifted a negligent shoulder. "There's nothing for me here in Seattle without you."

"Well, I'm not going anywhere without you," she'd told him.

"You don't want me with you on a date."

She'd laughed. "I'm not going on a date to Alaska."

"No, but you should visit before you move there. You could go next week, when I'm going on my class camping trip."

She'd stared at him. "I don't want to be gone when you are. I want to be here, by a phone if you need me."

"You have a cell phone," he pointed out.

"I'm not going to Alaska, Carlos."

He'd simply dropped the subject, a wise-beyond-his-years smile on his lips.

Katherine was left to obsess about it as she scrubbed. And scrubbed.

Alaska.

Vacuum, dust.

Alaska.

She'd never been, and had never really even thought about it. Now she could do little else. She was halfway through washing the kitchen floor when her doorbell rang. Thinking it was either UPS or her next-door neighbor, the very sweet Mrs. Jacobs with something homemade to eat, she swiped at her forehead with her arm and padded to the door.

But one look through the peephole made her gasp in horror.

Nick Spencer, Alaskan bush pilot, major good kisser.

Backing up, she stared at the door in shock, then down at herself. Her sweats were streaked with cleaner, and her tank top was wet in spots where she'd managed to spray herself with the showerhead.

He knocked again.

She dropped the scrub brush and smoothed her hair. *Hopeless.*

"Kat?"

Oh, Lord, that voice. It could melt the Arctic. It was certainly melting her resolve to stand still as stone and pretend she wasn't home.

"I can hear you," he said through the door with

such amusement that she had to stop and roll her eyes. "Your panicked breathing is giving you away."

"I am *not* panic breathing."

"Ah, she speaks."

Katherine groaned and leaned against the front door, which she had no intention of opening.

"You going to let me in?"

"How did you know I was here?"

"I went to the day care first. Open the door, Kat."

She looked down at herself and felt hysterical laughter bubble up. "Why?"

"To take you on another date."

*"Now?"* she squeaked.

"You know I don't have a lot of time left. I promised the girls I'd be home in a week, and half that is already gone. I can't disappoint them."

Her heart started a heavy drum. He needed a wife.

Soon. In a few days.

She couldn't be that wife. She had no business wasting his time. "What kind of date?" she heard herself ask.

"You'll have to open the door to find out."

In spite of herself, she laughed. God, the man was something.

"I can tell you this," he allowed. "It's on my terms today."

Oh, boy. *His* terms.

"You're going to like it," he vowed with that effortless confidence. "A lot."

Hmm. How would he possibly know? She opened her door.

He was either a very wise man or one used to facing women with wild hair and sloppy clothes, because he looked her straight in the eyes and said, "I'm going to have to insist you leave the gloves at home."

She looked down at the yellow cleaning gloves on her hands and gasped, then tried to shake them off, but the right one got stuck. Finally she yanked it off and crossed her arms. "I can't believe you got me to open the door."

He tugged on a loose strand of hair. "You're dressed perfectly for where I'm taking you. Grab a sweatshirt, and let's go."

"You're kidding, right?"

"Nope."

"Nick, I can't go out like this."

"Why not?"

She dipped her head down and looked at herself. "Because I'm wearing sweats from another decade entirely, not to mention my utter lack of makeup and—"

He ran his dark gaze down her body, then back up again, lingering a bit on her wet tank top, and when he met her eyes again, his were even darker.

"Trust me, you're perfect. But you'll need good shoes, nothing stupid."

"Um…" What were stupid shoes? "What exactly are we doing?"

"Dating. Nick Spencer style."

*Oh, boy.*

FORTY MINUTES later they got out of his Jeep in a world far, far from the city they'd just left. Here was the Olympic Peninsula, just west of Seattle, and the home of the Olympic Mountains. The area was diverse, containing a rugged coastline, prairies, forests, snowy peaks and one of the few temperate rain forests on the planet. Also located on the peninsula was the Makah Indian reservation, and near that was a state park, which was where they got out.

Nick pulled a backpack from the back seat and came toward her, looking mighty pleased with himself. "A hike should make me feel closer to home," he said. "Maybe a swim. Definitely lots of food, and we're not talking sushi here." He hoisted the pack and reached for her hand in a gesture so easy and natural she didn't think to object, even though he'd been manipulating her since the moment she'd opened her door to him.

The day was warm, so she'd changed into denim shorts and a sleeveless blouse. She'd combed her hair as well, taming it back into a ponytail, during which time Nick had paced her living room like a caged tiger. She knew this because she'd peeked out her bedroom at him to make sure he was really there and not a figment of her desperate imagination.

When she'd come out, his gaze had homed in on her like a beacon. "Ready?" he'd asked, and since she'd been a little shaken by how aware of him he made her, she'd done nothing but nod.

She was as ready as she could get.

Nick moved from the Jeep toward a free-standing route marker that had a large map plotting out the terrain ahead. He studied the thing for a moment, then turned to her with a smile. "Let's go."

Just looking at his tall, rugged form dressed in a T-shirt, jeans and boots had her body humming and ready to go all right. The light breeze lifted his hair from his face, which was actually open and relaxed and—stop the presses—close to a smile. "Being outdoors makes you happy," she said, and smiled when he appeared startled.

"Being outdoors is my life," he said simply, and led the way.

The trail he'd chosen was easy enough that they could talk while they moved farther into the wilderness, surrounded by the massive, towering peaks that blocked out almost everything else, including the sky.

"So, do you do this a lot at home?" she asked.

"Yeah, though at home my backpack is a lot heavier because Kayla sits in it. And my hands are always full. One for Emily, who's just gotten running down to a science and loves to make me chase her. Then there's Annie, always hiding behind a tree or a rock, just to terrify me." He turned his head toward her and grinned.

*Grinned.*

Katherine nearly had to sit down because her knees wobbled at the sight of Nick Spencer so happy and full of life. He'd been right—she was going to enjoy this. A lot. "You take the girls on hikes?"

"Actually, *hike* is a bit ambitious for what we do. We pack up, go about ten feet, have to stop for a snack break. Go a little farther, and have to stop for a diaper change. Go another little bit, then have to stop to examine an interesting bug or discuss what we're having for dinner. By then—and this is after maybe a hundred yards if we're lucky—we're just done in." He smiled again, and the sight thrilled her heart. "I'm thinking you'll be an easier hiking partner than I'm used to."

"When I first met you, I never thought I'd be out with you doing this, having fun."

"Why not?"

"Because you seemed a little…intense."

"I was not."

She laughed.

And he looked over at her, that sure and knowing smile in his eyes.

Everything within her reacted. Over and over again, he surprised her. Yes, he could be gruff, and yes, he was definitely rough around the edges, but that in itself was part of his charm. Because along with that roughness came an honesty most men didn't have, and a willingness to please, which, quite frankly, put her mind in the gutter, wondering how else he could please a woman.

He tugged lightly on her hand, bringing her back. "What are you thinking?"

"Um…nothing."

"Does 'nothing' always make you blush?"

"Well…" She looked up, past the giant, ancient trees to the patches of azure blue sky, then back to the ground, where her boots crunched on the fallen pine needles and twigs, trying to decide what to say.

He gave her hand another tug until she looked at him, and found his gaze steady and…hot.

"Just with you," she finally said.

He brushed her shoulder with his, but thankfully let the subject go.

They kept walking, winding their way up. The sun peeked through the towering trees, beating down on them whenever it could steal through, steaming the ground, the rocks, the fallen timber, making the day so glorious it almost hurt to breathe.

After a little while the trail forked, both paths vanishing into the woods. They turned off the main trail onto the smaller one to the right, and she glanced back a little uneasily. "I should tell you," she said, only half-joking. "I could get lost finding my way out of a paper bag."

"I read the map," he said. "I know our way back."

Again, she glanced behind from where they'd come, but every direction looked the same. *Deep cleansing breath.*

Then he led them off the small trail entirely.

*Double deep cleansing breath.*

"I don't suppose now is a good time to ask how many women you've abducted into the wilderness," she said with a little laugh.

He shot her a quick grin. Good Lord, he really had to stop doing that. Her heart couldn't take the sudden spikes.

"Nervous?" he asked in a low, sexy voice that dissolved any bones she had left.

"Yes," she answered frankly, nervous she was going to beg him to kiss her.

He stopped. His big hand rose, slid along her jaw. "Kat?"

She gulped. "Yes?"

"If you keep looking at me like that, we're not going to get much farther."

She struggled to make her expression inscrutable. "How's this?"

Looking extremely amused, he lifted a brow. "Are you hungry?"

"Um… Well…" Then she was staring at his back as he moved forward into a little clearing. Facing away from her, hands on his hips, hair blowing in the breeze, he surveyed the view, which was magnificent, she had to admit.

But what caught her eye more than the amazing temperate rain forest around them, so alive with birds and insects and stunning growth, was the man in front of her. His broad shoulders threatened the seams of his T-shirt, the lines of his smooth, sleek back were clearly delineated through the cotton. He hadn't tucked his shirt in, probably hadn't thought of it. His jeans accentuated his lower half, and though she'd never been a woman to gawk at a man's body, she was gawking now.

"Hear that?" He cocked his head. "Water." Turning back for her, he grabbed her hand and pulled her through the clearing until suddenly they were staring at a river, which, due to a fallen tree the size of her entire house, had created a natural pool. "Looks like heaven to me," he said, and tugged off his shirt. "Want to wade in? Or jump from that rock outcropping?"

She stared at him, and not just because he was

suddenly half-naked. He happened to be pointing to a "rock outcropping" that looked more like a cliff. It was off to the right, and was actually a series of cliffs, the lowest one approximately twenty-five feet high. Twenty-five feet *too* high. "Are you crazy?"

"We'll wade, I take it." Still holding her hand, he kicked off his shoes, waited until she did the same, then stepped into the water. "Practically a hot tub," he said.

She choked out a laugh as the water lapped at her feet. The *chilly* water. But then he pulled her farther in until the water hit their knees.

"You know how to swim, right?"

"Knowing how to swim and agreeing to swim are two different things entirely," she said. "And we don't have bathing suits."

She could tell by the look that crossed his face that it didn't bother him in the least. "Our clothes'll dry," he said. "Come on." He dove in.

And vanished.

The water was smooth, the day utterly silent, unless she counted the insects buzzing and the occasional bird's cry. "Nick?" She turned in a slow circle, and just when her heart had started a heavy, freaked-out beat, when she'd waded in to her chest, frantically searching right and left for any sign of him, arms encircled her from behind and tugged.

She fell into the water.

A good old-fashioned water fight ensued, and then, with some heavy coaxing, he got her to climb to the lowest cliff.

"I'm not jumping," she said, laughing, even as he pulled her to the edge. "Really, Nick. There's no way I'm going to—"

Her protest ended in a scream as he leaped, holding her hand, taking her with him.

A GOOD HOUR LATER, they sat on the shore, panting for breath, drying in the sun, laughing like children. Katherine tilted her face up to the sky and sighed with pure pleasure. "Now, *this* is a day off."

It took her a moment to realize he'd moved away to retrieve his backpack and take out a small blanket, which he set around her shoulders. Then, opening the backpack again, he pulled out cheese and apples, and a bottle of wine....

Had she really thought he didn't have a romantic bone in his body? And what was wrong with her that she was melting all over the simple gesture?

Then he looked over at her. In his eyes was good humor, and much, much more.

She swallowed hard. "A picnic."

"Hope you're still hungry."

"Always." She kneeled beside him, watching as he cut up a few apples, sliced the cheese. Poured her a glass of wine. Every movement he made was economical and to the point. No hedging, no guessing with this man.

When he lifted a piece of cheese to her lips, she opened her mouth.

His thumb glided over her lower lip, causing all sorts of interesting reactions from the inside out. "I think you're better at this dating thing than you let on," she said a little shakily, and since payback was fair play, she fed him a slice of apple, making sure to slowly touch his lower lip, just as he had hers, gasping when he pretended to bite her finger, then laughing, even as the reactions in her tripled. "Do you date a lot at home?"

"Nope." He chewed the apple. "Come home with me and I'll never date again. Happily."

He knew she wasn't going to do that, and somehow, the lightly made comment had her relaxing. "Tell me about your place."

"It's a log cabin. I built it about eight years ago."

She looked at him in surprise. "You did?"

"With my own hands." He held up his callused palms and wriggled his fingers. "It's only fallen down twice now."

She gaped.

He laughed. God, she loved that sound. "I'm kidding, Kat."

She blushed. "Oh." Of course he was kidding.

This was a man who either knew what he was doing or made it a point to find out.

"It's out in the middle of nowhere, my favorite nowhere, with a short runway in the distance for my plane."

"You love it."

"Yep."

"You miss it."

"Very much."

She thought about how he'd be going back to it, and soon enough wouldn't be missing anything at all. She thought about her city, and how at this moment, it seemed so far, far away. "Would you ever consider moving?"

He cocked his head and looked at her for a long moment. "Why?"

"It's a reasonable question, I think."

"Yes, if you're asking because of you."

Trust him to be so blunt. "I'm asking…because of me," she admitted. "Because I'd like to be able to see you again." There. He wasn't the only one who could be so open.

Regret crossed his rugged features. "I can't imagine living anywhere else, no. But if you'd come with me to see it, I figure it'd only take but a minute for you to fall in love with it as much as I have."

"Because I like the picnic?"

"Because you have a soul meant for the great

outdoors. Because you are an amazing woman, an adapting one, an open one... And because—"

"And because you need a wife."

A wry expression curved his lips. "That, too."

She sighed. "It's getting late. I have to get back for Carlos."

He stood up, too. Then took her hand and put it against his bare chest where she could feel the steady beat of his heart. "I'm glad you came with me today."

She let out a long breath. "Is this goodbye, Nick?"

"Not yet." He leaned in and gave her a quick, brain-cell-destroying kiss. "Not quite yet."

## CHAPTER SEVEN

CRACK OF DAWN the next morning, Nick's cell phone rang. Opening a bleary eye, he glanced at the hotel clock and groaned. Not quite crack of dawn.

Which meant he knew exactly who it was.

Annie Spencer, demanding, smart-as-hell four-year-old, owner of one-third of his heart. She'd recently learned how to dial his cell phone and had been doing so morning and night.

Slapping his hand down on the nightstand, he searched for the obnoxiously loud phone and brought it up to his ear. "Annie, darlin', it's not even morning yet."

"Daddy!"

With a sigh, he rolled onto his back and smiled in spite of himself. "What are you doing?"

"Calling you. You on your way home?"

He scrubbed a hand over his face. "Are you in the kitchen?"

"Right in front of the calendar," she said proudly. "With my marker."

"So you know I still have two days left."

"Nope. I crossed them out so you can come home today. Now. That's why I'm calling. Why aren't you here?"

He sighed with regret. "It doesn't work that way, Annie."

"Why?"

"Because time has to pass before you can mark the calendar."

"Why?"

"Because you're cheating time, and time can't be cheated."

"Why?"

"Because—" He groaned and sat up. "You know what? It's too early for the why game."

"Why?"

He groaned again. "Tell me how you're doing. How're Emily and Kayla?"

"They're *babies*."

"Emily is two, she's not a baby."

"Uh-huh. She's a big baby."

"How are they, Annie?"

"Well…Emily went pee in the pottie yesterday."

"She did? That's great." They'd been trying to get her to do that for months, but the stubborn little troublemaker preferred to go on the floor in the kitchen. Or the living room.

Or wherever suited her.

"She used a whole lot of paper and plugged the

toilet. The water went all down the hall. Leila got mad.''

Leila was too old to have to deal with this. The poor woman would have left Nick long ago if she didn't love his girls nearly as much as he did.

He stretched and got out of the bed. Naked, he padded to the window and looked out on downtown Seattle. He could see the Cascades, but he could also see the Space Needle and a huge metropolis.

What he'd give to be looking out his own bedroom window to nothing but nearly six hundred thousand square miles of wilderness. "What's Leila doing now?"

"Unplugging the toilet."

"How's Kayla?"

"Good. She took off her diaper in the store yesterday."

"How did that go over?"

"She was sitting in the cart all nudie naked, chewing on her fingers and drooling all over everything, and then, guess what?"

Nick was afraid to guess. "What?"

"She pooped! Leila got mad again, and Kayla laughed and pooped some more. She's so gross, Daddy."

Nick could picture this scene all too well, and would have asked to talk to Leila to send his heartfelt sympathies but at the moment she no doubt wanted a piece of his hide. A big piece.

"Are you going to bring me a present?" Annie asked in a very sweet little girl's voice that didn't fool him for one minute. She was a tyrant, a very *smart* tyrant.

"Don't I always?"

"Yes, but this time I want something big," she informed him. "Like…" She lowered her voice to a conspirator's whisper. "Like Mommy. I want her back, I want that really bad."

"Oh, Annie." His chest tightened, ached. "We talked about this. I—"

"Emily wants her back, too. I know she does. She can't really talk yet except for 'da-da' and 'no' and 'mine.' But she says 'momma.' I'm not sure about Kayla. All she does is poop and drool. But Emily and I want Mommy. You said she can't come back no matter how hard we wish, but we want her here."

He felt as if he'd swallowed shards of glass. "Annie—"

"I'll give up Christmas," she said quickly. "And the tooth fairy, too. I swear, Daddy."

She might as well just kill him, he thought, and he closed his eyes. "Baby, I'm sorry. She can't come back. I'd do anything to change that for you, *anything,* but she can't come back."

"Then *you* come back. Come back right now."

He drew in a shaky breath. She had no idea he was here for her, and for her sisters. He wanted them to have a mom just as badly as they wanted one.

"I'll make you a deal," he said, feeling raw to the core. "I'll meet you halfway, okay?"

"But you took the plane."

"No, I mean I'll come home a day early. Tomorrow."

"Yippee!" she cried in his ear. "Love you, Daddy!"

"Love you too, baby." He hung up and rubbed his aching chest. Then he tossed the cell to the bed, walked into the bathroom and cranked on the hot water.

As a compromise to his daughter, he'd now lost a day in the campaign to find a wife, but that would have to be okay.

Besides, he'd found the woman he wanted. He wanted Kat.

Now all he had to do was convince her she wanted him back.

KATHERINE'S PHONE rang early Saturday morning, too. Not quite crack of dawn, but close enough to have her frowning in worry as she answered it.

"Hey, sis."

Drew, her baby brother who wasn't a baby anymore. For so many years she'd taken care of him and her mother that it was still a natural urge to say "what's the matter," or "what can I help you with," but those things were no longer necessary. "Hi there. Why are you up so early?"

"I just realized it's almost Mom's birthday, and I promised to do the party this year."

"Yes. So…"

"So…can you help me plan it?"

She laughed as she walked past Carlos's bedroom, then through the kitchen and out the back door into her garden.

"What's so funny?" Drew asked.

She pulled on a pair of gloves and knelt at a row of bulbs she'd planted the week before. Thanks to the rain, she had enough weeding to fill the day. The weekend. "I was just thinking that now you're married to Julia, you didn't need me anymore, and here you are calling me for help."

He let out a wry laugh. "I'll probably always need you."

"That's what I'm afraid of," she said, still grinning as she tossed a baby weed onto a quickly growing stack. "What do you want me to do?"

"Um…everything?"

So maybe some things never changed.

After she got off the phone with Drew, her mother called, wanting to know if Katherine could take time to speak about the day care at a library function. Or somewhere. Quite honestly, Katherine's mind wandered from the moment her mother said, "Can you…"

*Can you…*

*Will you…*

*I need you...*

Pretty much her entire life had been lived for others. She was no martyr, but the truth was, until recently she'd never really thought about how much she gave to just about everyone in her life.

Except herself.

That's what the sperm bank thing had been about, she could admit now. An overwhelming need to do something for herself.

Ironic, then, that the reason she loved her work so much was that she was able to give to others through it. But lately it just wasn't enough.

The plans to adopt Carlos helped.

Going to Alaska with him to join Nick's family would help even more.

She stopped in her tracks, right in the middle of the row with a weed in each hand.

*She was thinking about it.* My God, she was really thinking about it.

Even more unsettling, Nick hadn't left her mind, not since yesterday when he'd dropped her off right in front of her house with another one of those quick but shattering kisses.

Okay, truth. He hadn't left her mind period; not once since she'd plowed into the back of his Jeep. How could he? He was a man unlike any other she'd ever met.

She admired his lifestyle; he lived his life exactly as he wanted. And until just this morning and

Drew's phone call, she would have said the same about herself.

But that wasn't true at all, not really.

She'd always wanted to see someplace other than Washington. Granted, she'd figured Paris or Rome, but Alaska...that would work, too.

She was really, truly thinking about going. Just for a visit, of course. Just to see...

"Katherine?"

The back door slammed and Carlos appeared at her side, wearing an oversized T-shirt, jeans slung down past the level of decency, and the hottest athletic shoes that his saved-up allowance would buy. "Pull up the pants, Carlos," she begged. "Please?"

With a roll of his eyes, he did. "Kissy face is at the door."

"Um...who?"

"The guy you plowed into? The one who's been putting a goofy smile on your face— That one." He pointed at her. "That smile right there."

"I do not have a goofy smile on my face."

"Really? Should I get a mirror?"

Now *she* did the eye-rolling thing.

"Alaska man wants to know if he can talk to you."

Was it even eight yet? She rose out of the dirt and brushed off her jeans. She patted her hair and glared at Carlos when he snorted.

"Not helping," he said, eyeing her hair. "Not at all."

"Gee, thanks." She moved toward the house, pretending her pulse hadn't started a heavy, unnaturally fast beat at the thought of Nick at her door. "Did you let him in?"

"You said not to let strangers in. Ever."

"Yes, but—"

"In fact, you've told me not to even open the door to a stranger." He shot her an innocent smile. "You've told me that a lot."

She shot him another look at they walked through the kitchen and down the hall. "You left him outside, didn't you."

"Just following the rules."

"Uh-huh." She opened the front door and found Nick propped against the porch post. He lifted his head and ran his gaze over her in that way he had, the way that never failed to set her hormones off. "Hi," she said, so breathlessly she winced.

"Hi yourself." He held out a small ceramic pot with a seedling in it. It was just a baby, and if she had to guess from here, she'd say it was basil.

The man would probably never think to bring a woman flowers, but he remembered she liked basil.

Darn if that didn't melt her heart as well as activate those pesky hormones. "Thank you," she said, and found her face hurting from the stupid grin she couldn't control. "Did you meet Carlos?"

Nick's mouth curved wryly. "Through the door." He offered Carlos his hand.

Carlos, a little taken back at being included so easily in such a grown-up manner, awkwardly shook his hand. "Um...sorry about that."

"Hey, a man's got to do what a man's got to do," Nick said.

"Yeah." Carlos smiled at him, then smiled at Katherine.

Katherine could have hugged him, and she could have hugged Nick for making Carlos feel important.

Some of what she felt must have been in her face because Nick stroked a finger over her jaw and smiled at her. *Smiled.* "I was wondering if you've got some free time."

"For what?" She ruthlessly bit her lip because she still sounded ridiculously like Marilyn Monroe. *Stop it. Calm down. He's just a man.*

"For...whatever you like." He shrugged. "Lunch out, movie, shopping—"

She laughed and he blinked. "What?" he asked.

"Nothing, it's just the look on your face when you said the word *shopping.*"

"Yeah, well, if you must know, I rate shopping up there with root canals," he admitted. "I just want to do something with you today, something you want to do."

The way he put her desires first, despite his unease in the city, touched her. How many people in her life had done that for her? She looked down at the cute little seedling, then back at Nick. "Carlos and I were going to go ice-skating. Want to join us?"

He looked at Carlos. "What do you think of that?"

Carlos lifted a shoulder in almost a perfect imitation of Nick himself. "Whatever."

"Teenage code for 'I don't care as long as there's food,'" Katherine translated.

Nick nodded. "Well, food is a priority."

Carlos laughed.

Katherine did, too, for no other reason than her world felt good, really good. Shocking herself, she reached out for Nick's hand.

He turned his face toward her, and further stopped her heart with the look on his face. There was a sadness there, a regret she didn't understand, but she couldn't tear her gaze away. "Carlos... Why don't you go get ready? We'll meet you out front."

"I'm ready now."

She never took her gaze off Nick. "Go get ready again."

"You just want to kiss."

"Two minutes, Carlos."

When the teenager had shut the door and moved away, she stepped closer to Nick's muscular frame. "What's the matter?"

His eyes were dark and fathomless. "I'm leaving tomorrow."

Tomorrow. Her stomach sank.

"Fair warning." He dipped his head, and his lips skimmed her ear when he spoke. "I'm upping the heat of persuasion."

Carlos opened the door and eyed them with interest. "Two minutes is up."

KATHERINE WAS still lacing her skates when she looked up and caught sight of Carlos and Nick racing along the outside of the rink.

Carlos was good. She'd taught him herself.

Nick was better. Smooth, fluid strokes with that long, leanly muscular body, every movement effortless.

And fast.

He whipped by her, Carlos not too far behind, and flashed her a look that did something to her breathing.

On the next lap, Carlos pulled ahead by a nose, whooping, even as he huffed and puffed for air. "I win!"

Nick drew up, breathing hard but evenly. "I'm out of shape."

Not likely. Katherine stepped onto the ice, looking at the two males in her life, and felt such a constriction in her chest she could hardly stand it. With everything she had, she loved Carlos. She was deathly afraid that under different circumstances, the tall, proud man standing next to him could also someday claim an equal piece of her heart. If he'd been looking for such a thing.

But he wasn't. All he wanted, all he needed was a partner, not the greatest love of his life.

He didn't even believe in such a thing.

A dead end, a little voice inside her said, while her heart silently railed against it.

Nick held out his hand.

The chasm between them gaped further than the mileage between here and Alaska, but if she let them, these thoughts would ruin their last hours together.

Their last day.

"Kat?"

Lifting her chin, she smiled and took his hand. "Let's go."

With a little tug, he hauled her closer, and when she might have fallen, he slipped his arms around her and made sure she fell against him.

"Oops," he said. "Sorry."

It made her laugh. *He* made her laugh. "You look anything but."

His arms tightened on her as he stared down into her face, suddenly so serious, so solemn. "What?" she asked, clutching at him in worry. "What is it?"

He slowly shook his head. "You're beautiful,"

he murmured. "So beautiful." And he put his mouth to hers in a slow, melting kiss.

"Ewww!" cried Carlos, whipping past them.

Katherine blinked up at Nick.

He just looked back at her, the music, the other skaters, everything else fading away.

"I'm going to miss you," she said, and he closed his eyes.

When he opened them, they were dark, unreadable. "I know," he said simply.

AFTER SKATING, they went to a movie. Nick bought them buckets of popcorn, gallons of Coke and candy before they proceeded into the darkened theater to watch the latest Bond flick.

Nick didn't care about the movie, but Carlos did, and he'd decided he liked the kid.

Carlos sat in the front row with two friends he met. Kat smiled up at Nick. "Where do you want to sit?"

He looked at the back row. It was empty. *Perfect.*

Kat laughed. "I can't see from way back there."

Seeing the movie hadn't been what he'd had in mind, but he settled for somewhere in the middle, and the movie turned out to be engrossing enough to keep his thoughts off what they could be doing in the back row.

Until Kat set her hand on his.

On-screen, Bond was getting into heavy action

with his sexy costar. Offscreen, Kat's fingers lightly played over his, and though her attention never wavered from the movie, his sure did.

When her hand dropped down slightly, settling on his thigh, he nearly leaped out of his skin. Again, her fingers tingled his leg until he was a bundle of tightly wound nerves.

Finally he grabbed her hand and held it still in his.

She wriggled her fingers and he looked over at her. "Are you trying to drive me crazy?" he whispered.

Her eyes widened. "What do you mean?"

Okay, he was an idiot. He'd completely misread her intentions. "Nothing." He turned back to the movie, and just when he'd managed to get back into the plot, her fingers started moving again, skimming over the skin of his arm, and then once again his thigh, until he was so tightly wound he could hardly stand it. "Keep doing that," he whispered, leaning over to sip from the drink they were sharing, "and I'm going to get you back."

Eyes on the movie, she kept doing it.

Thank God. He let his hand fall to her thigh, just as hers had to his.

Her breath caught.

*Good.* Lightly he trailed his fingers over her leg, up and down, down and up, until he felt the muscles in her body quiver.

Even better. He reached across her to grab some popcorn from the container in her lap, letting his arm brush the underside of her breasts.

She sucked in a breath, held it.

Oh, yeah. Now they were *both* out of their minds, and not in the back row, damn it.

# CHAPTER EIGHT

AFTER THE MOVIE they went for a late lunch. They were eating fish and chips along the wharf in an outdoor café when Carlos said out of the blue, "I want to hang at Mark's for a little while. Until dark?"

Katherine had just been looking at Nick, trying to laugh and talk, all the while thinking this was their last day. Much as she loved Carlos, a few hours alone with Nick worked for her.

"You can drop me off after we finish eating," Carlos said, jerking his brow up and down in an obvious matchmaking attempt.

Katherine smiled. "Stop it."

"Well, it is his last day...."

Katherine didn't want to go there, so she took a sip of water.

"Unless, of course," Carlos said, "you decide to go."

She choked.

Carlos smiled innocently and patted her on the back.

When she could breathe, she looked at Nick, and caught his yearning and desire for her to do just that, go to Alaska with him. "I can't just up and leave."

"Why not?" This from Nick.

"Yeah. Why not?" This from Carlos.

"Because…" *Yeah, why not?* asked a little voice in her head, the little voice that was unhappy with her life, that was unsettled and still missing something. The little voice that wanted more, wanted love, wanted a family, wanted…*Nick.* "There's the day care, for one," she said. "With Hannah working from home right now, it puts a lot of pressure on Alexandra and me."

"She could handle a week, right?" Carlos nodded to Nick. "I think she could handle a week."

Katherine knew she could. Alexandra had confided that she'd broken up with Griffin, which left her with a need to keep busy.

"And I'm gone all next week, camping with my class, so you wouldn't have to worry about me like you always do."

"A week would be great," Nick said. "Come check it out. See the sights, meet the girls."

Yes, but since she had no doubt she'd love it, love them, what then?

Carlos was watching her. "I'd move with you," he said quietly. "If you wanted me to."

Katherine took his hand. "You know we're a team."

Nick tested Carlos's bicep. "You'd be a great asset to me up there."

"Really?" Carlos bulged his muscle at that. "Cool." He stood up and tugged at Katherine's arm. "C'mon, give me a ride?"

YEAH, NICK LIKED the kid a whole lot, and as they dropped him at his friend's, all sorts of things went on in his head.

Such as what he and Kat could do with a couple of hours alone.

He sat in the Jeep while Kat walked Carlos into his friend's house, and thought of each and every one of those things, only to be interrupted by his cell phone.

"Big news," Steve said in a low, excited whisper. "You won't believe it. I'm at a coffee shop."

"There's a million coffee shops in Seattle, more coffee shops than people. Not exactly big news."

"I met a woman."

"That is news."

"And she has a friend," Steve said. "A friend who is young and loves kids and loves Alaska. And she's stacked to boot."

"Steve—"

"*Stacked,* Nick. Look, I know you think you've got it covered, but I just wanted to make sure, because this girl—"

"I've got it covered."

"She wants to meet you. She's got some fantasy about being a mail-order bride and—"

"Seriously, I've—"

Kat slid back into the passenger seat and smiled at him. Carlos was gone for a few hours, and she was looking at him with a smile and an unmistakable hunger.

"Steve, I've got to go."

"No, wait—"

From across the car, Kat held out her hand.

Nick took it.

"Nick?" Steve sounded a little breathless now. "Listen to me. You've got to—"

"Go," Nick said firmly. "I've got to go," and disconnecting, he brought his and Kat's joined hands to his mouth.

THEY DROVE to the mountains again, and parked near the same spot they had for their hike. They took the trail, moving at a faster pace this time.

"What's the rush?" Katherine asked halfway up, breathless, laughing at herself because Nick wasn't even winded.

"You'll see." Ruthlessly, he tugged her along. "Hurry or we'll miss it."

"I am hurrying." She gasped for breath, laughing again when he stopped so short she plowed into the back of him, her hands sliding along his warm, hard, sleek muscles.

She was quite certain he noticed she didn't pull her hands back as fast as she should have. As he turned and put his hands on her hips, tugging her closer, she was equally certain he didn't mind.

"You're going to distract me," he said into her ear, bringing out a set of goose bumps along her arms. His hands glided up her spine.

Pressing her face to his throat, she opened her mouth and playfully bit him.

His hands went still for one beat, then slid down again, past the small of her back this time, slipping even lower, boldly cupping her bottom, pressing her into what was a most unmistakable bulge behind the buttons of his Levi's.

The motion unleashed something within her, making her feel…shameless. So she bit him again, then licked the spot.

That ripped a rough groan from deep in his throat, and he drew back, his breathing uneven as if he'd been running.

The man hadn't been winded getting up here, and yet being with her this way did him in.

She liked that. She decided she liked that a lot.

"Don't." He closed his eyes but let out a low laugh. "God, Kat, don't look at me like that."

"Like what?"

"Like you want me to gobble you right up, because I will."

Since that huskily growled threat only made her

shiver and press closer, he gripped her shoulders and turned her around, away from him. "Look."

"Oh my God." Ahead of her, to the right, the trail dropped away, revealing a sheer cliff. The meadow below was at least two hundred feet down, but the beauty lay in the setting sun directly in front of them, over the Cascades. The sky burst into myriad colors—red, orange, yellow, purple—and it took her breath.

Behind her, he shifted closer, then slipped his hands around her waist. Nestling his jaw against hers, he let out a long breath, his eyes riveted to the scene before them. "It's something, isn't it? From my house, the view is even more amazing, if you can believe it. Annie thinks it's her own personal nightly show. She brings popcorn."

Katherine sighed at the image, and a sharp longing burst through her. "That sounds so perfect."

She felt him shift his gaze from the setting sun to her profile. "You could see it yourself."

Deeply attracted to the affection and other things she heard in his voice, she took her eyes off the sunset and looked up at him. No doubt—she'd fallen under the spell of her unorthodox Prince Charming, moved by the love he had for his daughters, the reverence he had for his home.

When he let down his guard, he showed an incredibly sensitive, kind, warm side she'd never have guessed at.

He was like her fantasy man, but more.

He was *real*.

Slowly the sun sank behind the white-capped, magnificent Olympic Mountains, and with every passing second, she was quite certain her heart sank, as well.

This was it.

When the sun was down, he turned on his flashlight. Slowly she shifted around to face him. "This is goodbye," she whispered. "Isn't it?"

"It doesn't have to be." Lowering his head, he kissed her, and this kiss was different from the others; longer, deeper, wetter, and with so much heart and soul in it, she felt her throat close, her eyes burn, even as she clutched at him and burrowed in for more. She never wanted it to end. She wanted to drown in him, in the warmth of his hands on her, the way his body fitted to hers, making her feel so cherished, so safe, yet utterly sexy.

"How can I feel this way after only a few days?" she whispered when they'd pulled apart for air. "It doesn't make any sense."

"The only thing that makes sense is you coming with me."

She stared at him. She'd always been the mainstay, the one who'd steered the steady course. All her life. She'd never done anything impulsive, ever.

She'd never even left the state of Washington, for God's sake.

He cupped her face and tilted it up, the growing shadows making his expression all but impossible to read. But she didn't have to see the look there to know what he was feeling; it was in every line of his body. "It's just a visit, Kat. No ties. You don't like it, you pack up and come back."

"Nick—"

He put a finger over her mouth. "A week. Give me a week, Kat."

Clearly tired of talking, he kissed her, hard. Kissed her until her heart threatened to bounce out of her chest, until she was clinging to him, trying to climb up his body to get closer, closer to the heat and strength of him, closer to the hands dancing over her body, making it sing.

Then he lifted his head so that their lips just barely touched. "I want you," he said, and kissed her again.

Her senses took over.

The taste of him, the feel of him exploded in her head like fireworks, leaving her a whimpering, clinging, desperate mass of need. "How do you do this to me?" she asked. "I'm out of control, Nick. Completely out of control, and after just a kiss."

"That was not just a kiss."

No. No, it hadn't been.

"Give me that week," he said hoarsely, and hauled in a gulp of air. "And I'll show you more, so much more."

She'd never done anything like taking off for a week to a strange place with a man she hardly knew, but there was a first time for everything.

She'd wanted to do something for herself, had known something was missing from her life. What if this was it? She couldn't let the chance pass her by. "Nick—"

He took her mouth again in another long, earth-shattering kiss. Being held against his body, feeling his hands roaming restlessly over her curves had the little voice inside her urging her to try the fantasy on for size.

If only for a week.

Seven days.

Carlos would be gone anyway…

"Nick—"

He kept kissing her, and might never have stopped if they hadn't been forced to break apart to breathe.

"I'm going to come with you," she said.

His eyes heated, ignited.

"I'll leave the business and Carlos in Alexandra's capable hands for a week. A week to live the fantasy."

"I don't know about the fantasy part," he said slowly. "But I'll do my best."

She was fairly certain he would.

And that he'd fit the bill just fine. "After the seven days—"

He shut her up with a kiss, which she didn't mind in the least. Thinking about what would come after would only tear her apart.

She would deal with it later.

Much later.

# CHAPTER NINE

NICK HAD NEVER been nervous flying before, never. But he felt nervous now as he stepped onto the tarmac of the small local airport where he'd had his Cessna tied down for the past week.

Walking toward his turbo-prop eight-seater for his preflight check, he calmed, soothed as always by the thought of flying.

Besides, his nerves had nothing to do with the actual flight, but who was coming with him. That Kat was right now, this very moment, inside the tiny lobby saying her goodbyes to her family and friends—because of him—humbled him to the core.

He'd started this whole thing as a hunt for a wife, and had ended up with something very different. He'd ended up with Kat's promise to come for a week and test the waters.

If she liked it, then what? Would she really marry him? Fulfill his needs? Needs that he had a feeling were changing.

He didn't want to think about that. Hell, he'd be thrilled if she stayed. And if this near chemical-like attraction was part of the deal, he'd figure himself the luckiest son of a bitch on earth.

He'd do his damnedest to make her feel the same.

Flight check complete, he settled up his bill for tie-down costs and fuel, then went into the lobby to get her. She was holding Carlos by the hand, smiling at Alexandra, smiling at her brother and his wife and their baby, looking so happy, so excited, she took his breath. Honest to God, he had to stand there and gulp in more air.

Then she looked up and saw him. Her smile brightened, if that was possible, and she might as well have reached in and pulled out his guts.

"Hey," she said, still smiling.

"Hey back." His own smile was utterly helpless. "You ready?"

WAS SHE? Katherine wondered. If she went by the pounding of her heart, she was one beat away from a coronary. "Ready." She hugged her brother and his family. She hugged Carlos one last time, so long and hard he pretended to choke.

"It's only seven days," he complained good-naturedly. "And I'm leaving tomorrow, too, for the school camping trip."

"I know." Much to his disgust, she kissed him noisily again, then turned to Alexandra.

"Don't worry," her friend promised softly as they hugged tight.

Worry? Her? Only over every little thing. She'd called her mother, who'd been shocked and dismayed at her decision to go to Alaska with "a complete stranger." No talking could convince her otherwise.

Her brother had encouraged her to find what it was she was looking for, and had even come to see her off to remind her of it.

And now all she had to do was finish saying goodbye to Carlos and Alexandra, and she'd be gone. She hugged Alexandra tighter. *"What am I doing?"*

"You're going. I'll get Carlos off on his trip," Alexandra promised. "And I'll worry about the day care and whatever else comes up. So just…go for it."

Alexandra was as good as her word, Katherine knew, and some of the pressure she felt eased at her friend's promise. "But I'm leaving you at such a bad time. Hannah still isn't back to work, you just took that obnoxious phone call from the FBI about Gary's past, telling you to leave it alone—"

"I'll be fine." Alexandra pulled back, her green eyes shining with deep emotion she didn't always like to admit to. "You just go. Go get your happiness."

"It's just a short visit. A week, that's all."

Alexandra glanced over Katherine's shoulders at

# *An Important Message from the Editors*

*Dear Reader,*

*Because you've chosen to read one of our fine romance novels, we'd like to say "thank you!" And, as a **special** way to thank you, we've selected <u>two more</u> of the books you love so well **plus** an exciting Mystery Gift to send you — absolutely <u>FREE</u>!*

*Please enjoy them with our compliments...*

*Pam Powers*

# How to validate your Editor's "Thank You" FREE GIFT

1. Peel off gift seal from front cover. Place it in space provided at right. This automatically entitles you to receive 2 FREE BOOKS and a fabulous mystery gift.

2. Send back this card and you'll get 2 brand-new *Romance* novels. These books have a cover price of $5.99 or more each in the U.S. and $6.99 or more each in Canada, but they are yours to keep absolutely free.

3. There's no catch. You're under no obligation to buy anything. We charge nothing—ZERO—for your first shipment. And you don't have to make any minimum number of purchases—not even one!

4. The fact is, thousands of readers enjoy receiving their books by mail from The Reader Service. They enjoy the convenience of home delivery...they like getting the best new novels at discount prices BEFORE they're available in stores... and they love their Heart to Heart subscriber newsletter featuring author news, horoscopes, recipes, book reviews and much more!

5. We hope that after receiving your free books you'll want to remain a subscriber. But the choice is yours— to continue or cancel, any time at all! So why not take us up on our invitation, with no risk of any kind. You'll be glad you did!

## GET A *Free* MYSTERY GIFT...

SURPRISE MYSTERY GIFT COULD BE YOURS ***FREE*** AS A SPECIAL "THANK YOU" FROM THE EDITORS

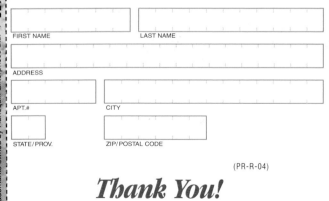

## The Reader Service — Here's How It Works:

Accepting your 2 free books and gift places you under no obligation to buy anything. You may keep the books and gift and return the shipping statement marked "cancel." If you do not cancel, about a month later we'll send you 3 additional books and bill you just $4.74 each in the U.S., or $5.24 each in Canada, plus 25¢ shipping & handling per book and applicable taxes if any.* That's the complete price and — compared to cover prices starting from $5.99 each in the U.S. and $6.99 each in Canada — it's quite a bargain! You may cancel at any time, but if you choose to continue, every month we'll send you 3 more books, which you may either purchase at the discount price or return to us and cancel your subscription.

*Terms and prices subject to change without notice. Sales tax applicable in N.Y. Canadian residents will be charged applicable provincial taxes and GST.

the big, restless, gorgeous man behind them. "Whatever you say, sweetie."

"I'll call."

"I've no doubt." Alexandra nodded to Nick. "You'll take care of her."

He turned his dark gaze on Katherine. "I will." In his eyes was an eagerness, an inner peace she hadn't seen in the days she'd spent with him, not even on their hike, when they'd been in his element.

Was she seeing it now because he was finally going home, or because she was going with him?

He clasped Carlos on the shoulder. "Thanks for sharing her with me."

*Because she was going with him,* she thought with no little amount of awe, her breath catching. He was happy because she was going with him. She'd given him this.

Then he held out his hand to her, and suddenly she saw other things in that amazing gaze of his.

Such as the things he wanted to do for her. To her.

Somehow that made it even more difficult to breathe. So did his touch. Anytime he put his hands on her she came a little unraveled. He had that way of reaching in and turning her on without any effort at all.

She was crazy. She didn't know him, not really. She had no idea what he'd expect out of her, if he'd—

"You're thinking too much," he said as they moved to the lobby door, still waving.

Yes. Yes, she was. Suddenly they were outside. It was one of those overcast Seattle spring mornings. The air hung so wet that dew dripped off everything, but it hadn't started raining.

They stepped onto the tarmac, headed toward his aircraft, which seemed sleek and mysterious. Just before they climbed in, Nick slowed. Grabbed her hand.

"You're shaking, Kat."

"Nerves." She shot him a smile that must not have fooled him because he moved close, close enough that his body blocked out the view of the opened door waiting for her to step in and leave behind everything she'd ever known.

"Want to change your mind?"

She looked into his dark, intense eyes, searching for…something, and found reassurance, affection and…need. "No. I don't want to change my mind."

"Good." He nodded, assuming she'd spoken the truth. It would never occur to him that she wouldn't.

And she had spoken the truth. But an extremely small part of her was still whispering in her ear that she was crazy.

"You're still thinking too much," he said.

"I can't seem to help it."

"Carlos is going to be fine, he's a great kid. Alexandra seems to have a great head on her shoulders.

You've got your brother and his wife watching your house and your garden—''

''I know.''

''Look, Kat…'' He skimmed his fingers over her jaw, sank them into her hair in a gesture so completely sweet, yet at the same time sexy, that her body quivered. ''I want you to want this,'' he said.

''I do—*I do*,'' she repeated more firmly. Because he seemed to need it in a way that made him stronger not weaker, she gave him a hug, then smiled up into his face. ''You want to know a secret?''

''Yes.''

''I've never left the state of Washington before.''

His jaw dropped. ''You're kidding me.''

She shook her head.

''Well, no wonder you're jittery as hell. I thought it was me.''

She laughed. ''Oh, it's you, too.''

He slowly shook his head at her.

''I mean, what if you turn out to be the perfect man in the perfect place and I never want to go home?'' she whispered.

He went utterly still. ''Well then, I'd fly you back to visit your family and friends anytime you wanted me to. The end.''

Her heart constricted. ''Yeah.''

He helped her into the plane. She'd never been in one before, and this was smaller than she'd expected. But the inside was clean, cozy and safe—she hoped.

"Okay," she whispered to herself, buckling in. "I can do this."

"You sure can." He sat next to her and put on a set of headphones. Then he turned to her, gave her one of his rare but heart-stopping smiles, and put his hand on her thigh. "Ready?"

With his hand on her, she was ready for anything. She covered his hand with hers. "I am now."

"Is that because I've already started the engine and it'd be embarrassing to have to back out?"

"Yes. But it's also because you touched me." She smiled at his obvious surprise. "It's quite a soothing touch you've got there, Nick."

"Uh-huh."

He didn't look convinced, and she laughed. "Hasn't anyone ever told you they like your touch before?"

He started flipping switches on the control panel as he thought about that. "No."

"Well, I do," she said softly, her heart revving when he looked at her, his eyes heated.

"Kat—"

"Are we going to sleep together, Nick?" she whispered.

"God, I hope so."

Her tummy fluttered. Her nipples hardened. And in between her thighs, all sorts of things happened.

"If I'd come with you as your wife, would you have expected that?"

"I didn't really dare to go that far with my expectations. Then I met you." He shifted uncomfortably. "Kat—"

"I'm just wondering if that would have been one of the...*duties*."

He let out a rough bark of laughter as he continued to work the controls. "Duties? Baby, when we sleep together, 'duty' is going to be the last thing on your mind."

*When we sleep together.* She held her breath, tried that out for a thought, and decided it just made her feel like a boneless heap of need.

"You're going to love the view." And with that, he took them down the runway and up into the air.

Her thoughts of hot and torrid sex were momentarily set aside as she gripped the sides of her chair and watched out the window with a mixture of terror and exhilaration.

Lift-off was louder than she'd expected, and she sat incredibly still, but the plane held together and they actually lifted into the air. In less than two minutes she had her nose to the glass, watching Seattle fade away from view. Goodbye Space Needle. Goodbye Puget Sound and Mount Rainier. Goodbye San Juan Islands.

Goodbye home.

When nothing but the dark blue Pacific Ocean

stretched out as far as she could see, her mind shifted back to hot and torrid sex with shocking ease. She turned to watch Nick fly. Did he have any idea how sexy his large hands looked on the controls, his expression one of intent concentration? "Are we going to sleep together *tonight?*"

He cut his glance her way, his eyes nearly hidden behind his aviator sunglasses. "That's not quite the question I expected. I thought you'd want to know how long the flight was, or how I charted our course. Or if there's an on-flight meal planned. Something like that."

"Are we, Nick?"

He blew out a breath. "Is 'damn I hope so' the wrong answer?"

She couldn't help it, she let out a nervous laugh.

He put a hand on her thigh. "I've told you I want you, Kat. What I haven't told you is that I want you in a way I'm not used to wanting."

Her heart melted. Her erogenous zones stood up and started panting. "Really?"

"I've taken more cold showers in the past week than when my hot water heater blew out last winter."

She laughed again, less nervous now, and he sliced her another long look. "You find my...discomfort funny?"

Her eyes on his, she had to swallow hard at the simmering heat in his gaze. Her humor faded and bloomed into something else entirely. "No," she whispered, and licked her suddenly dry lips.

He groaned and shifted in his seat. "Oh, that helps."

She bit her lip. "Nick…"

"Yeah?"

"I was just thinking, I'm not sure anyone has ever wanted me quite like this."

"I'm sure that shouldn't turn me on," he said, squeezing her leg. "But it does."

"Have you ever…in a plane?"

"You mean join the mile-high club?" he asked, lifting his brow.

Just the way he said it made her knees weak. Could they really make love while he was flying? Of course they couldn't, she decided, glancing at the tight seats in the back. And it wasn't as if he had autopilot or anything.

"Kat." His laugh was rough. "Your thoughts are all over your face and you're killing me."

She covered her suddenly hot cheeks. "Sorry." Subject change, quick. "So…how do you plot the course?"

With a knowing smile, he told her.

But she still thought about the mile-high club all the way there.

WHEN THEY FLEW over Anchorage, with the expanse of the Alaska Range just to the north, Nick felt an excitement hum through his body.

They were nearly home now, his home.

"It's so much bigger than I thought." Kat was glued to the window. "And so...commercial."

"It's the largest city in Alaska," he said. "It's the hub of the state, at least commercewise."

"And the mountains..." Shaking her head, she took in the range spanning in front of them as far as the eye could see, topped and covered with a coniferous forest that unfurled like a green ribbon across the horizon. "So beautiful. I almost feel like I'm at home."

"I'd hoped so." He banked the plane, turning eastward.

"How much farther?"

"Just a few minutes. Those there? They're the Chugach Mountains. My house is at the base of them." The mountains he pointed to stretched out from Anchorage, encompassing the front of Prince William Sound. Thousands and thousands of square miles of wilderness.

His backyard.

"The Chugach Mountains," she repeated softly. "Sounds lovely."

"It is awesome scenery. Just north are some amazing tidewater glaciers. I can show them to you while you're here if you'd like."

"We can drive there from your house?"

"Fly."

She stared at him. "Do you just get into your plane like I would my car?"

"Pretty much."

"Wow." She eyed him as if she found that idea incredibly sexy, and he had to say the same about her response.

"This area is famous for fishing, especially halibut," he said. "Ever been?"

"No, but I like halibut." She shot him another side glance that made him want to howl at the moon. "Nick?"

Oh, man, that voice. He'd probably agree to anything if she kept talking to him in that voice, the one that said he made her just a little bit hot. "Yeah?"

"Will you teach me how to fly?"

Okay, amendment. He'd agree to anything but that. No one flew his plane. "Uh..."

"That would be so exciting..."

Aw, hell, he was a dead man. "Kat—"

At the look on his face—pure horror, he was sure—she burst out laughing. "You don't know how to say no to me, do you?"

He grimaced, rubbed his jaw.

"Nick, that's dangerous knowledge," she said softly, then grinned. "Real dangerous."

THE VAST PANORAMA beneath them was speckled by myriad lakes and bogs left by the glaciers, a view

Nick never tired of. As they came in for a landing, he glanced at Kat. "Ready?"

She gave him a smile. "Ready."

He nodded and started their landing, wondering where this week would lead.

When the plane came to a rumbling stop, Kat looked out in wonder, then back at him. "Nick, my God. I'm in love."

His heart jerked once, hard. She was talking about the landscape around them, of course, the wide, majestic mountain range, the sea of pine trees, junipers and wild grass. His cabin was just a short way off in the distance. "Yeah. It grows on a person."

He helped her out. She waited until he finished shutting down the plane, until the tie-down was complete and they were ready to head to his cabin before putting a hand in his. "I mean it," she said quietly.

He squeezed. "I'm glad."

They headed toward his house, which he tried to look at as a stranger would. The structure was only about 1900 square feet, but he'd made the most of every inch. Log cabin style, he had two chimneys, both of which were smoking now, meaning Leila was chilled again. The woman's arthritis was getting bad, bad enough that she dreamed of moving to Cabo San Lucas, where she could be warm all year round.

The windows were bare but the land around had been cleared of the bush indigenous to the area. Wildflowers had been inadvertently planted, courtesy of his four-year-daughter, who'd spilled a bag of seed two years ago.

It had been an early thaw and a wet spring, so no snow dotted the ground as it usually did this time of year. Instead, new growth had already popped up, and all around them as far as they could see was green, green and more green.

The house was situated in the middle of all this glory, his log cabin, with his entire life in it, and he never tired of coming home to the place.

They walked through a meadow of wild grass toward it, and he didn't miss the flutter of movement behind the kitchen windows.

His time was limited, seriously limited.

"Oh, Nick, look at all this land. It's…awe-inspiring."

He glanced around them and inhaled the unique scent of Alaska. "It is that."

"And the house…it's just so beautiful." Within twenty feet of the house, she stepped on the well-worn path leading to it. "Just beautiful."

And so was she. Patience gone, he hauled her into his arms.

"What—"

He stopped whatever she might have said with his mouth, deepening the kiss when she gasped, moaning when she lifted her arms and fisted his hair in her hands, arching into his body.

Always when he had his hands on her and his tongue in her mouth, rational thought escaped him, and right now was no exception. He kissed her until his eyes crossed with lust and vicious need, and only when it was keep kissing her and suffocate did he lift his head.

In his arms, dazed and sexy as hell, she stared at his mouth while she slowly licked her lips, as if she had to have that last taste of him.

It made him groan again.

"What was that for?" she managed to ask.

"Trust me." He let her go and grimaced at the discomfort of his jeans. "There won't be time for another of those for far too long to suit me."

"What do you mean—"

The front door of his cabin opened. A screeching whoop sounded, and then they were mobbed by his household.

# CHAPTER TEN

AMONG THE SQUEALS and jubilant cries of ''Daddy, Daddy!'' Katherine stepped over the threshold of Nick's house and felt engulfed by the strangest sense of homecoming.

It was silly, of course. This was just a visit. Just one little week. She glanced back at Nick, needing a little balance in a world gone off-kilter, and found him engulfed by two little girls who'd thrown themselves at him.

With one child in each arm, limbs all entangled, wet kisses everywhere, Nick didn't look anything close to the tough and edgy man she'd first met on a rainy street in Seattle. He didn't look dangerous or rough and tumble at all.

He looked utterly and completely human.

Even vulnerable.

And when he closed his eyes and buried his face between the girls' faces, something deep within her softened. Melted.

Yearned.

''I missed you so much,'' he whispered in a voice

that brought a lump to her throat. The love on his face was almost more than she could bear, and though she wanted to turn away, she couldn't.

She'd had moments like this with her father, before he'd gone to jail when she'd been six.

Nick turned in a slow circle, still hugging his daughters tight, their little bodies looking so fragile and yet safe in his arms.

"You feel good, Daddy."

"You feel good, too, Annie." With a smile he lifted his face and touched his nose to the older child's, gently rubbing back and forth.

"Inuit kisses!" she screeched, and returned the favor before cupping his cheeks in her little hands and giving him a smacking kiss on the lips.

"Me! Me!"

Obliging the younger one, Nick turned his head and gave her the same nose rub he'd given Annie.

She giggled. *"Dad-eeeee."*

Nick's entire face softened at the adoration in that single word, and Katherine would have sworn his eyes went suspiciously damp. "Yes," he said in a rough whisper. "Daddy's home, Emily."

Torn between the need to run far and fast, and the reluctance to take her eyes off the man she was suddenly and deathly afraid she'd fallen for, Katherine swallowed hard.

But Emily just grinned from ear to ear. "Dadeeee,'' she said again, clearly smitten. ''Daddy, home. *Daddy.*''

Katherine smiled. The toddler had likely used her entire vocabulary in that one sentence.

An older woman stood aside, waiting. Leila, Katherine figured. She was of Tlingit descent, with a wrinkled, weathered face the color of fine leather. She wore thick black leggings, fur boots and a long sweater with a scarf over her head. She held a baby, the ten-month-old Kayla.

Nick lifted his head and smiled at Leila. ''Hey.''

''Hey yourself.'' She thrust the baby out at him, and he actually managed to grab her while still holding Emily and Annie.

Snuggled in his arms between her sisters, Kayla blinked huge eyes up at her daddy, then let out a toothless smile, accompanied by a long line of drool.

''That's my girl,'' he said, and kissed her noisily on her chubby cheek, making her giggle, too. Then he turned to Katherine. ''Are you ready for this?''

She smiled through her tight chest. ''You bet.''

''Okay.'' He looked at each of his daughters. ''Annie, Emily, Kayla...this is Katherine.''

Annie stared at her. ''Why?''

''Because that's her name,'' Nick said. ''And Katherine, we have here Annie, Emily and Kayla. All happy to meet you.''

''Hello, girls.'' Katherine stepped close and

smiled at each of them, her heart tugging just a little because they were all so adorable, each in her own way. All three girls had dark, long hair, and Nick's equally dark eyes. Annie's were filled with reservation, but not Emily and Kayla, who were so clearly in heaven in Nick's arms.

"Katherine's going to stay for a week," Nick said, and Leila sighed in relief.

"Good. You found one. See you." She headed around him toward the front door.

"Where are you going?" Nick asked.

"Off to my sister's. You won't need me for a week—unless you screw up. Don't screw up," she said, and vanished.

FOR TWO HOURS Nick listened to the girls' tales of the week. Actually, he listened to Annie, who could talk the ear off a saint, but Emily nodded her head often, and Kayla drooled, ate her fist and all around supported her sisters by dozing. They sat on the floor by a roaring fire in the living room.

Or rather, Nick sat on the floor and the girls sat on him, treating him like their own personal jungle gym. Katherine had offered a lap as well, but Annie had politely refused her, and after that, of course, Emily had done the same. Katherine had tried to take Kayla, but once the little one realized her sisters were still with Nick, nothing else would do for her, either.

So Katherine sat across from them, watching Nick with a smile on those lips he wished he could lean in and kiss again. What was she thinking?

And did it involve body parts?

Leila was long gone, so he needed to think about dinner, but Annie wasn't done with him. Yet if her story went on for much longer, his eyes were going to glaze over.

"—and then Emily bit the ear on that stuffed animal you gave to Kayla," she continued. "The one you won at the carnival? And then Kayla cried, and then—"

"Annie." He had to laugh. "Aren't you tired of hearing your own voice yet?"

"Nope. And then—"

"Snow!" Emily pointed to the window, and all of them turned their heads in surprise.

"Rain." He rubbed his hand over Emily's long, tangled hair. "That's rain, squirt."

She climbed off the couch and waddled on her short little legs to the window. "Out. Daddy, out."

"You want to go out in the rain?"

Smiling her agreement, she ran to the door.

"Yeah, let's go sing in the rain!" Annie cried, moving toward her sister. "Like last time, Daddy, remember?"

He remembered. About a month ago, he'd been working on his plane, with the girls playing in the grass behind him. An unexpected rainstorm had hit, and before he'd known it, the girls had taken off their clothes to roll around in the mud. He'd waded in to get them and had ended up on his ass in the mud as well, which they'd found hysterically funny.

"Dance in the rain," Annie demanded, and came back to the floor to tug him up.

He pulled Kat up with him. "I think we're going dancing in the rain."

She smiled at him, but for the first time, the smile didn't quite meet her eyes, and something akin to panic filled him.

Did she want to go home already? Were the girls too much? Was it all too much? "What is it?" He held her hand when she would have drawn away. Helping his cause, Kayla, still in his arms, reached out and grasped a fistful of Kat's hair.

"You're caught," he murmured. "Now talk to me."

"Daddy! *Rain!*"

"Coming, Emmie." He kept looking at Kat. "What is it?"

"You're wanted for a dance in the rain," she said softly.

He searched her features, needing a clue, needing to know what had spooked her. It wasn't Kayla, not when Kat looked at the baby with nothing less than naked joy. The woman was a natural mom, whether she knew it or not, and he suspected she did.

So what had happened? "Kat?"

"I'll wait here," she said. "Do you want me to cook dinner?"

She didn't want to intrude. *Was she kidding?* He'd brought her here to intrude, to integrate herself into his life, to be a part of the girls, to be a part of everything. "No, I don't want you to cook dinner. You're not here to serve us. Come on, Kat, we're wanted for a dance in the rain." He thrust Kayla in her arms, and the baby smiled a toothless, wet grin up at Kat. *There,* he thought. *Just try to resist her.*

"Uh…"

He simply grinned down into Kat's face, kissing her on the nose the way his daughters had kissed him.

Kat stared at Kayla.

Kayla stared back at Kat.

Nick wrapped an arm around Kat's waist and headed toward the door. "Let's go." He grabbed up Emily and reached for Annie's hand. "Grab Kat's free hand, would you, Annie?"

"Don't we need jackets?" Kat asked, blinking out into the rapidly fading daylight.

"Jackets? Nah." Nick grinned. "You don't melt, do you?"

"Well, no, but—"

*"C'mon."* Annie reached for Kat's spare hand, and together, all five of them stepped out into the rain.

The moment they did, Annie let go of their hands and set off running, arms out, screaming like a banshee. Surrounded by wild grass and tall, towering pines, she tossed back her head and opened her mouth to catch the drops in her mouth. "Caught one!"

Emily squirmed to be let down, so Nick let her go, too, and she raced toward her sister, her mouth already open.

Nick pulled Kat close.

Kayla rested between them, and might have even reached for her daddy, but Nick leaned in and set his head on Kat's shoulder.

Kayla eyed him, then slowly, watching Kat very closely for her response, did the same to Kat's other shoulder.

Nick sighed and snuggled his face in closer.

Kayla watched solemnly, then slowly repeated his gesture, snuggling as close to Kat as she could get.

Kat's eyes softened, and her hand came up to cup Kayla's small head, which was covered in unruly fine baby hair.

Kayla let out a sound of pleasure, a little coo, and Nick watched his daughter wrap Kat right around

her little pinkie finger with ease. *Atta girl, Kayla.*
"How are you doing now?" he asked.

"Good." And this time when she smiled, it
reached all the way to her eyes. "We're getting
wet."

"I like wet."

Kat's eyes flashed heat. "You're bad, Nick Spencer."

"Nope. I'm good." He made sure to flash the
heat right back at her. "Very, very good." And with
any luck, he'd prove it to her. Tonight.

DINNER WAS a family affair, Katherine discovered a
little bit later as they gathered around the large
wooden table in the kitchen.

"I didn't build a dining room," Nick had told her
when she'd helped Annie set the table. "Seemed
like a waste of space when we spend all our time in
the kitchen or the living room."

Katherine had to agree. It certainly gave the place
a more homey feel to have the kitchen and living
room open to each other, with high ceilings and
wood floors, one great perfectly sized space for three
little girls to run wild in.

The furniture was well battered, but large and incredibly comfortable. Two couches and a recliner in
the living room, and the large block table in the
kitchen. That was it.

The floors had been covered with throw rugs that were constantly crooked or piled on top of one another to make a "magic carpet," as Annie so helpfully explained. "We all sit on the carpets and go see Momma."

"Oh." Katherine felt a hard pang at what these three little girls had been through, so early in life. "I bet she loves that."

Annie beamed at her, but the smile faded, and she scratched her head, looking down at her toes, one of which was poking through a pink sock.

Katherine kneeled on the floor and looked into Annie's face. "You okay?"

"Sometimes I want her to come play with us."

Katherine put her hands on the girl's thin arms and managed a smile. "You know what I think? That she loves watching you play from heaven."

"She probably misses us a lot."

Katherine might not have lost a parent to an untimely death, but for much of her childhood she had lost her father. She liked to think she could understand Annie's hurt and bafflement. "I know it." She smiled and stroked Annie's cheek. "Who wouldn't miss you?"

"Yeah." Annie looked around, then satisfied no one could overhear her, she leaned in. "Do you think she's watching me all the time? Because sometimes I pull Emily's hair." She was so serious, so heartbreakingly serious. "Just when she takes my stuff, you know? And when she lets Kayla drool on it, but I don't want my momma to see that."

The lump in Katherine's throat grew. "Oh, sweetie. I'm thinking she understands perfectly. But maybe you could try hard not to get mad at your sisters, or to keep your good stuff up higher. Your mom would be so proud."

Annie nodded. "'Kay."

Unable to help herself, Katherine pulled Annie in for a hug. That the little girl allowed it made her feel as if she'd won the lottery.

"Gotta finish setting the table," Annie said after a moment, and pulled away. "Daddy!"

Nick stood in front of the stove, dumping a chopped onion into a large pot that was beginning to smell like heaven. "What?"

"I need more napkins."

He started cutting up a green pepper. "I'll get them for you. Do not—" He lifted his head and pierced his daughter with a long look. "Do not climb up the shelves like you did last time."

Annie's eyes widened. "I wouldn't do that." She clasped her hands and recited verbatim what Katherine suspected was a recent lecture. "The whole thing could come tumbling down on me," she intoned. "Crush me like a grape. Flatten me out like a pancake."

Nick dumped the peppers into the pot and glanced at her again. "Just don't climb."

"'Kay." She vanished.

"She's going to climb," he muttered. "She's a goddamn monkey."

"She's the smartest little four-year-old I've ever met."

"You mean she's a smart-*ass*."

Katherine laughed at his wry tone, which held a good amount of confusion in it. Poor, poor man. Out of his league already.

Nick was wielding the knife as if he'd cooked plenty of dinners in his time, and given his upbringing and current lifestyle, she figured he had. Fascinated by the sight of a man moving around in the kitchen with such ease, she stood even closer, peering around his shoulder. "What are you cooking?"

"Something I'm hoping will halfway resemble chili." He wiped his hands on a towel and eyed her. "How are you at making cornbread?"

"Oh, I will, I will!" Annie had reappeared and was jumping up and down. Emily, who would probably follow Annie to the ends of the earth, eyed her sister's actions for a moment, then started to mimic her, jumping up and down as well.

"Me, me," she shouted.

Kayla was in a high chair at the table, watching her sisters. She lifted both her hands as if to say "me, too!"

Katherine laughed. She scooped up Kayla and grabbed Emily's hand before turning to Annie. "What do we do?"

"You mean...I'm in charge?"

"Well, how does that sound?" she asked the little girl.

Annie grinned. "I like to be in charge."

"Well then, Queen Annie, lead the way."

Annie lifted her nose high enough to get a nosebleed and bowed.

Nick groaned. "Don't encourage her."

"Oh, your poor daddy." Katherine cuddled the utterly cuddlable Kayla closer. The baby had her fist in her mouth and was drooling around it, but never took her wide, dark beautiful eyes off Katherine, making her feel...whole. "I think he's feeling outnumbered," she whispered.

"That's because he is," Annie pointed out. "There's three of us girls and only one boy." She eyed Katherine very solemnly. "With my mommy, there used to be four."

Once again Katherine kneeled down by the girl. "Is it okay with you if there's four now, for just a little while?"

Annie looked at Kayla, who had set her head on Katherine's shoulder, and Emily, who still held her hand. "Yes," she whispered. "For just a little while, we can have four again."

## CHAPTER ELEVEN

AFTER DINNER, there was a whirlwind of little girl baths, teeth brushing and storytelling. By the time Annie and Emily were in their bunks—Annie on top—and Kayla next to them in her crib, thumb in her mouth, Katherine was ready for bed herself.

"Exhausting, isn't it?" Nick stood with her in the open doorway of the girls' large bedroom, shirt plastered to him from the baths. He was also coated with several dabs of bubblegum-flavored toothpaste.

She looked up at the big, tough man, the one who could be brought down by a sloppy kiss from any of his three amazing daughters, and found herself giving him a silly smile. "I'd say exhilarating."

"Hmm…you have an odd sense of exhilaration." He stroked a finger over her jaw. He smelled like a combo of toothpaste and strawberry bubble bath. His five o'clock shadow, which appeared to be at least a few days' growth of beard, reminded her of how it felt gliding along the skin of her throat.

And just like that, her silly smile turned…hungry.

"Whatever that thought is," he murmured, "hold

on to it.'' He took her hand and carefully, silently backed them down the hall and into the living room.

He took her to the hearth and knelt before the glowing fire, then tugged her down next to him. Face-to-face, he lifted a hand and sank his fingers in the hair at the nape of her neck. ''So. Here we are.''

''Yes.'' She smiled.

''You survived your first day in the untamed wilderness of the Spencer household.''

''That I did.''

''What did you think?''

What did she think? That his daughters were already under her skin. Annie with her smart observations and heartbreaking need to remember her mother, Emily the happy troublemaker and daddy's girl and especially Kayla, who'd responded to her with a warm, loving innocence she still couldn't think about without her eyes stinging.

But mostly, there was the man in front of her, who in his element had turned out to be the most masculine, sexy man she'd ever met.

Her every dream come true.

Oh yes, she could fall for him, for the girls, for his Alaska. But though he was incredibly loving toward his children, and wildly, overtly sexy toward her, he didn't expect love to fit into the equation when it came to needing a wife.

And she wanted, needed that love.

Looking at him now, knowing what she did about the way he'd grown up, about what his marriage had been…she wondered how to make him believe in love. "I think you have the most wonderful little girls," she said. "And that they take after their daddy."

His fingers tightened on her and drew her closer so that their mouths were only a fraction of an inch apart. "I'm going to kiss you," he whispered. "It's quite possible I'm going to kiss you all night long."

*Oh, please,* was her only thought as she leaned in to close the distance herself. His deliciously firm, warm mouth touched hers, and she shuddered out a breath because this—*this*—was exactly what she'd been yearning for since the moment she'd seen him grab his daughters for a welcome home hug.

Both his hands came up and held her face now, and she grabbed his wrists, wanting more, deeper, wetter, and he was all too happy to oblige her. They strained against each other, arms and hands fighting for purchase, his slipping under her sweater, hers exploring his broad chest and shoulders.

"Daddy?"

Nick went still, then let out a heartfelt groan in Katherine's ear.

*"Daddy!"*

"Yes," Katherine said with a laugh, and pulled back to find Emily standing right at their sides, her little "blankie" in one hand, her daddy's shirt hem in the other to get Nick's attention. "Daddy is right here," she said. "What's the matter, sweetie? Can't sleep?"

"Daddy home."

"I sure am, kiddo." With a sigh, Nick stood up and scooped the little girl against him. Reaching a hand down for Katherine, he pulled her up, too. His eyes were hot, his hand still warm from her own flesh, and his breathing wasn't close to steady. "Whenever I come back from an overnight trip, she likes—hell, *demands*—to sleep with me," he explained.

She wanted to laugh at the look of utter sexual frustration on his face, but since her entire body was humming with his promised pleasure, she couldn't muster even a chuckle. "I understand."

"We're not done," he growled in her ear.

She hoped not.

"Maybe she'll fall right back to sleep," he said hopefully. "And then…"

Oh yes, and then. Katherine leaned in to kiss Emily on the cheek. She smelled like the same strawberry bubble bath her daddy did, and was warm from her bed, making Katherine's heart turn on its side. "Sleep well, Emily, 'kay?"

"'Kay." Emily smiled sleepily and then did something to shock them all.

She opened her arms to go to Katherine.

Katherine divided a startled look between twin dark gazes. "Can I?" she whispered to Nick.

"Are you kidding?" He let Emily climb into Katherine's arms. The little girl promptly put her head down on Katherine's shoulder, stuck her thumb in her mouth and closed her eyes.

Her dark hair tickled Katherine's nose, her little fingers lay trustingly against her chest.

And Katherine's heart expanded.

"Take my bed," Nick whispered, walking them down the hall and opening his door, then waiting until she stepped over the threshold toward the huge four-poster bed. "And, Kat…"

She turned back to him.

He tucked a strand of her hair behind her ear, rimming her lobe with a finger and drawing shivers of desire down her spine. "If she falls right asleep, I'll be here…"

At the trailed off words, her body went back on hopeful, humming alert. "Then so will I," she whispered.

KATHERINE WOKE UP the next morning to her cell phone vibrating on Nick's nightstand. She glanced at Emily, who for a tiny little thing had nearly all of the king-size bed, both pillows and most of the blankets.

And snored like a buzz saw.

With a soft laugh, Katherine grabbed the phone

and saw that her caller was Alexandra. "What's the matter?" she said, automatically kicking into worried mother mode. "Is it Carlos?"

"I just dropped him off for his trip, and I'm sure he's fine," Alexandra said quickly. "I didn't mean to scare you."

"It's okay." She glanced at Emily, who lay on her back, arms and legs sprawled out. Katherine let her fingers run over her little rounded belly.

With a tiny sucking noise, Emily rolled over, sticking her well padded bottom in the air and her thumb in her mouth.

"I'm sorry to have to tell you this now—" Alexandra drew a deep breath "—when you're trying to take a well-deserved vacation, but we have a problem. A big one."

"Uh-oh." Still, it wasn't Carlos. She figured she could handle anything else. "What is it?"

"First, promise you won't panic and come back."

"Just tell me."

"Promise me first."

Alexandra was quite possibly the most stubborn woman on the planet, Katherine knew. There'd be no getting anything out of her until she did as she asked. "I promise. Now tell me."

"You'll finish your week up there?"

"Yes, but you're scaring me."

"Jordan Edwards died."

"Oh, no." Katherine sank her head back to the

pillow and stared at the ceiling. *"Oh, no."* Jordan Edwards was a very old friend of the family, and the sweetest, kindest man Katherine had ever met. He'd been the one to loan her a very large chunk of money to open the day care—interest free, no due date. She didn't have any sort of balloon payment either, just a simple monthly payment, which she'd managed to pay every single month without making much of a dent in the debt. Jordan hadn't minded one little bit. That was the kind of man he'd been. "How?"

"A stroke."

She closed her eyes. "I hope he didn't suffer."

"No. But…" Alexandra let out a slow breath. "His heirs are calling the loan. Immediately."

"What?"

"We both know we don't have the money to pay it off."

No, they didn't. Nothing even close. Katherine stroked her hand down Emily's back and tried to push her thoughts past Jordan's sad death to think how it was going to affect them. "Okay. I'll come back tonight—"

"No. No way. You promised."

That she had. And in any case, what could she do other than panic? Besides, she didn't want to go home. Damn it, she wanted to stay here and see this out. "We can raise the money."

"How?"

Emily, still out like a light, snuggled closer. "Let me think…" She gathered the little girl to her and sighed. She'd meant only to wait until the little one had fallen asleep before seeking out Nick again, but whether it had been the flight, or all the emotions, she'd hit the pillow and that had been it.

And missed out on a night in Nick's arms.

Emily let out a long, loud sigh of content, and Katherine smiled. She'd been looking to connect with Nick, but here in bed with Emily, she thought maybe she'd connected with him on another level entirely.

"Katherine?"

"We'll work this out, somehow. Another investor maybe, or several." None like Jordan. He'd been one of a kind, but surely there was someone else. Or a grant or…something.

Alexandra let out a frustrated breath. "We need a miracle."

"Hey." Katherine sat up. "Did I ever tell you about that time I helped out at bingo night for Carlos and his eighth grade class?"

"Bingo? Honey, we're not talking a couple of hundred dollars."

"We made two *thousand*. But listen. I'm just thinking we do something like that on a bigger scale. A much bigger scale, say, like…a benefit auction."

"A benefit auction…" Even Alexandra, ever the

doomsayer, couldn't keep the hope out of her voice. "You know what? That just might work."

"I'll get started on it."

"No," Alexandra said firmly. "No way. Your job is to forget about it for now. You came up with the plan, I'll get going on it. Besides, if I have my way, we'll have it scheduled and worked out by the time you get back."

And she would. The woman was a virtual pit bull when it came to protecting what she cared about, and she cared about the day care, just as much as Katherine did. Thank God she wasn't alone in this. "Promise you'll call me later. Tell me how it's going, and what I can do from here."

"What you can do from there is try to forget our troubles for now, and have fun with that gorgeous hunk of a bush pilot."

"Alexandra." Katherine laughed. "I can't just—"

"Seriously. I only called because you'd have been pissed if I hadn't. Otherwise, I'd never have interrupted what I'm hoping is a great, fun, *extremely* hot time. Now go back to it. That's an order."

Katherine shook her head, still smiling. When she tossed the cell aside, she looked up to find Nick standing just inside the bedroom door, watching her.

"Everything okay?" he asked softly.

He'd just gotten out of the shower, if his wet hair and bare chest meant anything. He wore only low-slung jeans and an expression that made breathing difficult.

*Was everything okay?*

She wanted to say *oh, yes*. Despite the grief over Jordan, despite fears of getting the money she needed to pay back the loan, right this very second, everything was so okay she could have burst. She had the man of her dreams looking at her as if he wanted to gobble her up.

That wasn't all she wanted from him, but she thought being gobbled up was a darn good start. And if the rest came, well then… "I'm so sorry about last night. I can't believe it, but I fell asleep—"

Pushing away from the wall, he walked toward the bed, stopping only when his knees brushed the mattress. "I know."

"You do?"

"After a while, I came looking for you."

The barely banked heat in his eyes made her suck in a breath. "Why didn't you wake me?"

"Because you had Emily all curled up with you." Humor came into his gaze now. "And you were both snoring loud enough to wake the dead."

That bubbled a laugh out of her. "I was not."

His lips quirked. "You looked so exhausted I didn't have the heart to wake you."

Ah. She'd looked exhausted. Not sexy, not wild and passionate. Not even desirous.

Exhausted.

He tugged lightly on the sheet covering her until it came free, exposing her in the tank and panties that she'd left on after stripping off her jeans and sweater. "And while you also looked…" Trailing off, he eyed her body from head to toe, and let out a long, ragged breath. "*Amazing* in my bed, I had to walk away or I'd have woken up Emily."

Oh. *Oh.* She'd looked amazing? Amazing worked for her.

"But tonight—" he tilted his head and studied his slumbering daughter with a fond half smile "—no kids in the bed."

No kids in the bed. Oh boy.

"So…" He ran a finger over her belly, making it quiver. "What's the matter?"

"Oh…" She sat up, feeling sadness well at the reminder. "An old family friend passed away."

He grimaced. "I'm sorry."

"Yeah. Me, too." She sighed. "There's also… some work stuff."

"Are you wanting to go home?"

She looked at the blissfully sleeping Emily, then back at Nick. "No."

"Good." He cocked his head and studied her in a way that left her torn between wanting to tug her tank down to cover more of her, or pull it off over her head and toss it across the room.

"You up for an adventure?" he asked.

Given her body's response, the answer was an emphatic yes.

"Leila just showed up to watch the girls for us for a while." His lips curved. "Thought I'd show you some sights."

"Leila came back? I thought she was done with you."

"Apparently she realized she can't be done unless I convince you to stay. With that vested interest in mind, she's in the kitchen waiting. What do you say?"

She swung her feet out of bed. "I say you sure know how to take my mind off my troubles."

He eyed her pale peach tank top and panties in a way that had her bones liquefying and her thighs quivering. Swallowing hard, she backed toward the bathroom. "I'll just...shower and be ready in no time."

His eyes were dark and hot and right on her when she shut the door. Alone, she turned to look at herself in the mirror and fanned her face. The man made her positively smolder.

There was still the bone-deep sadness for Jordan, a real fear for Forrester Square Day Care...and an even deeper fear for herself and her emotions when it came to Nick. She should probably drop everything and go home, but...she couldn't.

Not until she knew she could fly home and never look back.

She took a hot shower, and despite the melancholy the call had brought, found herself smiling as she moved down the hall toward all the noise in the kitchen.

The three girls were awake and seated around the table eating eggs and toast. Leila nodded at her from her perch in front of the stove. "Make the most of this day, you hear me? Because—"

"Leila," Nick said while pulling juice from the fridge.

She merely waggled her wooden spoon in his face. "You, I'm not talking to."

"You will be if you scare her off."

Katherine smiled. "I'm not scared. And I'll make the most of the day, Leila, I promise. Thank you."

"Good. And you." Leila thrust the spoon toward Nick again. "Do I need to tell *you* what to do today?"

"I think I can manage." Nick poured the girls some juice, then leaned down and kissed Annie. "Be good."

"When are you coming back?" she wanted to know.

"Before your bedtime."

"'Kay."

He kissed Emily, then Kayla, both of whom reached out for a kiss from Katherine, too.

Her heart nearly overflowed. She couldn't just kiss them, she had to hug them, so she pulled each one up into her arms for an extended quick cuddle, then turned to Annie, who affixed a look of disinterest on her face.

That Katherine could see right through it nearly broke that overfilled heart, and despite the child's expression, she kissed and hugged Annie too, nearly bursting into tears when Annie sighed and hugged her back. "See you later," Katherine whispered, and followed Nick out.

They were silent as he led her to the garage. When he held out a helmet, gesturing to a large all-terrain vehicle that looked lean and mean, she lifted a brow.

"Four-wheeling," he said. "It's the next best way to see the landscape after my plane." He checked the strap on her helmet, and his long fingers touched her jaw as he did, causing an interesting set of shivers to race down her spine. She figured he didn't notice, but then he left his hands on her much longer than necessary, and she looked up into his face.

"You have the softest skin," he murmured, and leaned in, putting his mouth on her throat beneath the helmet. "Yum."

Her knees buckled, and she let out a little laugh. "Here, Nick?"

"No." He swung a leg over the quad and gestured for her to do the same.

She did, wrapping her arms around his waist so there wasn't enough space between his smooth, hard back and her much softer front for even a thin sheet of paper. Wriggling just a little to get comfortable, her thighs spread to accommodate his, she felt each and every erotic zone in her body tingle.

She smiled a little grimly when his muscles bunched and tensed in response, but then he revved the machine, and drove them off into the wilderness.

They rode for a long time, up a steep trail, down another, and farther on, until they came to another trail. One side was granite rock, leading so far up into the sky she couldn't see the top. The other side was a sheer drop that made her hold her breath in both terror and exhilaration.

But there was nowhere she'd rather be. Tipping her face up to the sun, feeling Nick's strong body handle the machine with practiced ease, she sighed in pleasure and let the day—and Nick—take her.

FINALLY HE SLOWED the quad, then stopped entirely, idling the machine on top of the world. Or at least his favorite spot in the world.

They had a 365 degree mouth-dropping view of magnificent mountains and wide open Alaskan wilderness as far as the eye could see. Far below lay a blanket of forest, dotted with lakes and rivers and creeks. Up high, surrounding them, was a small meadow filled with tall natural grass and new wildflowers in every hue under the sun. "How are you doing?" he asked Kat.

"Great." She climbed off the quad, removing her helmet when he did the same. "What now?"

"Typical city woman. Always in a hurry." He took her hand. "There's no hurry here, Kat. Just you and me and the hours of the day stretching in front of us."

Her mouth curved. "You never fail to surprise me."

"How is that?"

"That first day, when I crashed into your Jeep? I'd have sworn you were a rough, edgy, slightly terrifying man, without a whimsical bone in your body."

"And now?"

"And now..." She let out an amazed laugh. "You make me melt, all the time."

"Melting is good, right?"

She laughed. "Haven't you ever melted, Nick?"

His eyes never left hers as he considered that. "I melt every time I look at you," he said truthfully.

"You see?" She pointed at him. "You're doing it to me again, right now."

Enough to make her want to stay? "There are some caves not too far from here," he said. "Dating back to ancient Indian times. Want to see them?"

"I'd love to."

He grabbed his backpack in one hand and kept

hers in his other, taking her down a short path that led to a series of rocky caves jutting out from nowhere that he'd been lucky enough to find on a little jaunt with Annie a month or so back. Because he was used to having little kids with him, he had a blanket in the pack. They sat on it in the sun at the opening of the cave, their backs to the rock, their fronts to the most incredible view of Alaska he'd ever seen, and he'd seen plenty.

A large bird soared forty or fifty feet overhead in crystal air, hovering a moment before fluttering down with a clear melodious trill. Again and again the ritual was repeated.

"That's beautiful," Kat breathed.

"He's a Lapland longspur," he said, watching her watch the bird with avid interest. "He's trying to impress his woman."

"I hope it works."

"It will work. See?" He pointed to the bird as it dived to meet another, smaller longspur.

Together they soared off into the day.

He pulled out a soda from the backpack and offered it to Kat. "I'm sorry again about your family friend."

"Thank you." She stared down at the can and sighed.

"Tell me what's happening."

"It's too pretty out here to talk about my problems."

He scanned the horizon, then looked at her. "This is a perfect place to talk about problems. Nothing seems insurmountable here."

"Nick—"

"Look, Kat, you gave up a week for me. Do you have any idea what that means to me? More than I can tell you, believe me. Now you're worried about something, something big, I can feel it. So spill. I want to hear."

She just looked at him.

He skimmed his thumb over her full lower lip. "Come on."

"It's just that…" She bit that lower lip, dragging it across her teeth, and he went inappropriately hard. "You…want to be there for me," she said quietly.

Aw, hell. He dragged his mind out of her pants. "Aren't there people who are there for you, Kat?"

"Usually, *I'm* the one people lean on."

"So take a day off." He stroked her jaw, watching his touch affect her pulse. "And lean on me."

With another sigh, she told him about the loan, the fears that they wouldn't be able to cover it if the benefit auction idea failed and how that would be the end of the day-care center that meant so much to her.

"The benefit is a good, solid idea," he said. "And the more patrons you get to donate things to auction off, the better, right?"

"Yes."

"Then I'll donate a free tourist flight around Seattle to check out the sights."

"Oh, Nick, that's so sweet, but you don't have to—"

He kissed her to shut her up. Not that he didn't want to talk some more, or hear what she had to say, but he wanted to kiss her more than any of that. In fact, he pretty much wanted to kiss her more than he'd wanted anything in a long time.

Her hand came up, her fingers snaking through his hair to hold him in place.

As if he was going anywhere!

Then she fisted her other hand over his chest, and his heart kicked hard.

Slowly, her fingers slid down, stopping his heart in its track when she got to his jeans. He waited, not breathing, but she didn't go farther south.

Instead, she slid her hand beneath the hem of his sweatshirt, gliding her fingers up past his stomach...from pec to pec on his bare flesh. His every muscle leaped to hopeful attention. "Kat—"

She gave him a sleepy-eyed look that was the sexiest thing he'd ever seen, and slowly glided her hand back down, down...her finger dipping in his belly button.

She was coming on to him.

A little stunned by that, he caught her hand in his so he could think. "Maybe you should tell me what you're doing, so I don't make a complete ass of myself guessing.''

"I'm doing what you think I am," she whispered, and leaning in, she bit his earlobe, making his entire body jerk. "I want you, Nick." And then she soothed the spot with a kiss.

She wanted him. Thank God. He took her mouth again in a long, wet, deep kiss, the hunger building, killing him. It wasn't enough, it'd never be enough, and only in part because he'd been so damn lonely, so damn afraid he'd always be that way. The loneliness wasn't new, nor was the urge to bury himself in a woman to keep it at bay.

But actually, he hadn't been with anyone in a very long time. Pulling back slightly, he held her face between his hands.

"I want you," she said again. "Do you want me back, Nick?"

He nearly laughed, but ended up groaning instead. "More than my next breath," he said simply, and reached for her.

# CHAPTER TWELVE

MOUTH ON HERS, Nick pulled Katherine into his lap, leaning back against the opening of the cave.

"Good?" he murmured.

"Very."

With a purposeful intent in his gaze, he lowered his head toward hers again, letting his hot, open mouth drag up her throat this time.

Her breath caught.

"Mmm." He nibbled his way over her collarbone, nudging her sweater aside as he went. "Love that sound."

She'd definitely aroused him, and had done it on purpose. She'd wanted him so badly, had wanted to show him, to express her feelings in a way he'd understand. He drew her in ways no other man had. Yes, he was different. He was more physical than she'd imagined. He was unpolished, and rough around the edges.

And she wanted him just the way he was. "Here, Nick?"

He covered her breast with his wide palm. "Oh yeah. Here."

She arched into his hand. "N-now?"

"Definitely now." He peeled off her sweater, then unbuttoned her sleeveless blouse, pushing it aside. Her bra was white and lacy, and he seemed to appreciate the look of it, at least for the second it took him to flick open the front hook and skim it away from her. With characteristic bluntness, he looked his fill, and in that moment she experienced her first doubt.

She'd wanted to drive him wild. Shower him with heat and affection, show him what it could be between them. But she didn't know if she had what it took to— Oh my God, he cupped her bared breasts and glided his rough thumbs over the tips, making her hum with helpless pleasure. "Nick—"

"Oh yeah. I love it when you say my name like that." Another slow glide of his thumbs, and his name was ripped from her throat again, making him groan. "Just like that," he said thickly, "all breathless, with that little quiver in your voice. Sexy as hell, Kat." He bent over her and flicked his tongue across her right nipple.

With a gasp, she arched up, right into his mouth. "Mmm," he said, his mouth now full. She slipped her arms around his neck as he pulled her closer, but the full physical contact brought no relief, just more desperation and need. He was strong and hard and so into holding her, touching her, she could feel him trembling, too.

He pulled away long enough to lay her back on the blanket, then he took her face in his hands and kissed her until she could think of nothing else but the raw, carnal need shimmering between them.

It never occurred to her to slow down, or to want a bed, not during the wild kisses, or when he rose up to unzip her jeans and slide them off her legs. Making love with Nick outside, surrounded by his glorious element, by Mother Nature at her finest, seemed more perfect than she could have imagined. He touched her with his eyes, then his hands, and finally with his mouth, his open, wet, hot mouth, driving her nearly out of her mind with his tongue, his teeth, before leaving her a sobbing, panting wreck on the blanket so he could tear off his own clothes and lower his body back down next to hers.

He started all over, patiently, slowly, again stirring the desperation, the unrelenting need. The power of him, and the heat, didn't surprise her, but the grace and tenderness did as his magic hands took her to just the point of release, and then again with that giving, talented mouth… Before she'd caught her breath, he'd covered himself with a condom and slid home, deep inside her.

Her surprised little gasp of pleasure mingled with

his quiet "oh, yeah." She should have known how shattering this would be, since he'd already shown her what an incredibly physical, passionate, sensual man he was. His fluid moves and bold thrusts took her completely beyond herself. With effortless ease he brought her to the edge again and held her there, lifting her away from the woman she knew herself to be, making her as earthly, as wildly passionate as he.

Crying out his name, she dug her nails into him, letting go of everything but this, being able to do that because he was right there with her, kissing her, murmuring his encouragement, letting her know he was as lost in this as she was. At the end, he reared back, driving her even higher, then higher still, and when she shattered, shuddering in his arms, he threw back his head, her name on his lips as he followed her over.

NICK LAY on his back in the sun next to Kat, watching the clouds go by. "I've always wanted to do that here," he said.

"You mean…you've never…here?"

She sounded so shocked, he expended the energy to lift up onto his elbow and look down at her. God, she was beautiful, all long and willowy in the sunlight, so beautiful he couldn't help but touch her again. With a hand on her belly, he leaned in a little closer. "Never," he whispered against her lips.

That provoked a purely feminine smile that shot straight to his groin.

"I think," she said quite smugly, "that I like being the one."

The one. Hell yeah, she was the one.

A thundering sound had them both sitting up.

In the valley far below, a few hundred scattered caribou, many of them young calves, were stampeding through the wild grass together.

In a moment came the answer why, when a large, dark animal ambled over the crest of the far hill. A big, hungry, brown bear with paws the size of a grown man's head and teeth capable of tearing into anything. Typically, bears wanted less to do with man than man wanted to do with them, but Nick knew enough to respect the territory, and he watched carefully.

Kat gasped when she saw it. "Ohmigod, he's huge. And fuzzy."

"Yes, a big fuzz ball. With teeth. It's a grizzly. A hungry grizzly."

"Should we move?"

"He's not after us at the moment."

They watched him lumber downhill, after the caribou.

But then suddenly the large beast stopped short.

He just stood there on the valley floor, on his back paws, lifting his nose in the air, wriggling it right then left.

Without warning, he started running in the opposite direction, back from where he'd come.

"He caught our scent," Nick said. "And clearly didn't want anything to do with us."

"That's a very good thing."

"Yep." God, she was so damned sexy with that drowsy, sated, cat-in-cream smile. Leaning in, he kissed her, and she kissed him back, and in no time there was nothing lazy or drowsy about what was happening to his body yet again.

His hand glided down her, over a curved breast, her belly, between her legs. She was ready for him, and he was certainly ready for her. There seemed to be a starved spot deep inside him, a starved spot for her, for everything she did, and being with her like this fed it.

"Again, Nick?"

God, yes. "Again." He grabbed a condom and rolled with her so that he lay flat on his back, with Kat sitting astride him, her hair falling over her shoulders, and when she leaned down to kiss him, it also fell over his shoulders and chest. Her pebbled nipples brushed his, making him tremble. *Tremble*.

She took the condom and sheathed him. Then she lifted herself up, just enough that the very tip of him slid into her, and he gripped her hips and let out a hungry groan.

"This, with you," she whispered, her eyes half-closed in ecstasy. "It's different."

It was different. Hot, earthy. *Desperate*. He'd just had her and he wanted her again with a biting need he hadn't anticipated.

"Different. And deep." Her eyes opened on him, questing and just a little unsure. "I know it's barely been a week, but…this feels right, doesn't it, Nick? It feels…enduring."

He opened his mouth, though he had no idea what the hell he was going to say, but she sank onto him so that he was buried to the hilt inside her glorious body, buried and snug and hot and… "Ah, hell." Pulling her down for a long, hard kiss, he nearly died when she began moving on him.

"See?" she murmured thickly in his ear. "It's different."

It didn't take a rocket scientist to figure out what she was trying to tell him. She cared for him, a lot. Possibly…loved him.

"I mean *good* different, you know," she said, clearly thinking she needed to explain.

But he wasn't ready for the explanation. And certainly not for…*love*. Yes, he felt differently toward her than he had anyone else, including his late wife, but hell if he knew why.

He looked up into her soft, glowing face and felt his heart constrict.

Damn. He did know why.

But it wasn't what he'd expected to happen here. All he'd needed was a mother for his kids, and maybe a woman to care about him, as well, one who'd warm his bed at night, without the words and emotions.

Words and emotions weren't necessary.

*But she's warm and loving and needs the words and emotions, you idiot, and you should have seen that coming from a mile away.*

And maybe he had, and selfishly he'd wanted her anyway, or even because of it. But now he wasn't sure he had what it would take to make her happy.

And even if he did have it, it didn't matter, because he'd never use emotions against her to make her want to stay. He wanted her to stay because...

"Nick—"

Surging up, he kissed her. Yes, he did it to keep her from asking questions he couldn't answer, but also because he couldn't get enough of her. With his mouth on hers, his hands on her breasts and his erection stretching her to full, maybe, just maybe, he could try.

QUITE A BIT later, Kat sat up and looked down at him with her riotous hair and a saucy, smug smile on her face. "I'm going to have a very fond spot in my heart for this place," she murmured.

"Yeah. Me, too." In fact, he doubted he'd be able to walk past this cave again without getting an erection. With a groan, he sat up and looked over his body. Amazingly enough, he was still in one piece.

She smiled. "Did you feel it, too, Nick?"

"Oh, I felt it. All the way to my toes."

"I mean—"

"Wait—" He cocked his head. "Hear that?" Around them was complete and utter silence. "I think you scared all the birds off with your cries."

She blushed, and pushed him. "I wasn't *that* loud."

He lifted a teasing brow. "Are you sure?"

Her smile faded. "You're good at that."

"What?"

"Changing the subject."

Yeah. Yeah, he was. He turned and looked into the valley.

"Nick." At her gentle tone, the one that told him she no longer was in a sexy, playful mood, he shifted his gaze back to her.

"It's okay," she whispered. "You don't want to talk about your feelings, I get it."

"Kat—"

"No, really. It's okay."

He searched her face, having enough experience

to at least know that her words had big lie potential, but she looked as open and as genuine as always.

"I don't want to rush you," she said quietly. "That wasn't my intention at all. It's just that…how I feel about you tends to burst out of me at odd times."

"Yeah." God, she was the most understanding woman on the planet, and what was he in return? An ass. "I don't want to disappoint you, Kat. And I really don't want to hurt you, but honesty is everything to me. I know no other way. And while I can tell you I think you're an amazing woman, that you make me feel good, you make me laugh, you make me…*happy,* and believe me, that's quite an admission coming from me—"

"I know. Nick, I know."

"I just don't have a lot of faith in that whole love thing, and—"

"I know." She reached for her clothes. "It's okay."

"Kat—"

"Take a breath, Nick." With a smile, she reached her hand out to him. "I get it. You want to just concentrate on today, on the here and now, and that works for me. Because if we're being honest…?" She put her other hand on his chest, just over his heart in that sweet gesture she had, the one that always brought him to his knees. "My here and now is pretty darn good."

"Yeah. So's mine." He touched her face, tilting it up for a kiss that unbelievably stirred him again.

She curled into him, snuggled in, fitting his body as if she'd been made for the spot.

*Fool*, an inner voice said. *Tell her you're feeling everything she's feeling, and quite possibly more. Do it.*

He opened his mouth.

Then closed it.

And instead, took her yet again.

## CHAPTER THIRTEEN

LEILA GREETED THEM at the door, and in fact blocked their way with her ample body. Hands on her hips, she eyed Nick first, looking him over slowly from head to toe and back again, taking in his wild hair—which the helmet hadn't helped any—his wrinkled shirt and the red spot on his throat where Katherine had bit him in the throes of passion.

She still couldn't believe it herself, but she'd left her mark on him. Torn between horror and thrill, she clamped her lips together and managed to keep her half-hysterical giggle to herself.

Then Leila turned that sharp gaze on her. Katherine stood up a little taller, but she had a feeling she didn't look any better than Nick, that what they'd done was all over their faces, never mind their bodies.

Good thing her neck and chest were covered, because Nick had left his own marks. Her body tingled just remembering exactly how he'd given them to her.

And she wanted to do it again.

"Humph," was all Leila said.

Nick craned his neck, trying to see inside. "What are you hiding?"

"What are *you* hiding?"

"Oh, for Christ's sake." Nick sighed and tipped his head skyward before looking down at Leila. "What do you want from me? You told me you wanted time off, I got you time off. Now you're here again, still bossing me around. Tell me what the hell to say to you."

"You can start with telling me how you did today."

"I did good," he said with mock politeness. "Now can we go in?"

"Sure." Moving aside, she eyed the bite on his neck and smirked knowingly. "I thought I told you to always wear bug repellent."

"Funny." He passed her and pulled on Katherine's hand.

But Leila stood in her way, a considerable deterrent in the narrow doorway. "Let her go, big guy. We're going to have a little chat. Woman to woman."

"Leila—"

"Oh, go greet your little ones, Nick." Leila shooed him along.

"Go on," Katherine said when Nick hesitated.

She could hear the girls getting all excited inside. "They can't wait to see you. I'll be right in."

Nick turned a steely gaze on Leila. "If you scare her off now, you'll be stuck here forever," he warned her. "Remember that."

"Oh, go on with you." Leila pushed him inside. Then looked at Katherine.

It took all Katherine's effort not to shift her weight, but even without the telling gesture, she knew she looked guilty as hell.

But Leila's knowing smirk was gone. In its place was a worry she hadn't let Nick see.

"What's the matter?" Katherine asked her, automatically reaching out for the older woman's hand. "What is it?"

Her fingers were thick with arthritis as she squeezed Katherine's fingers back. "You're a sweet girl. I'd hoped so, but I can see it in your face. I'm just so relieved." She searched Katherine's face for a long moment. "But more than that, you care about him."

"Yes," Katherine admitted softly. "Very much."

"Then nothing's wrong, nothing at all." She moved out of the doorway, and the two of them watched Nick being attacked by his three daughters in the living room.

He tossed Annie up in the air, catching her amid

squeals and demands for more. He tossed Emily next, and her little grin tugged hard at Katherine.

"You like his girls, too," Leila whispered.

Katherine's heart sighed when he reached for Kayla, tickling her rounded belly until she burst out in laughter. "Oh, yes."

"I can't tell you how happy I am to know this."

"Because if I stay, you're free to go?"

"Because if you stay," said Leila, "it'll be for love." Her voice and eyes softened as she took in Nick, with Annie and Emily on his back and Kayla in his arms. He paraded them around the living room, their happy squeals and coos filling the house. "He's so full of love, my Nick, but he's never had anyone love him back." She looked at Katherine and now her eyes were just a little damp. "His first wife, she'd had a rough life, much the same as Nick. She just wanted kids and a house, and Nick could give her that. She cared about him, in her own way, but she didn't love him. Not the way he deserves to be loved."

Yes, he did deserve to be loved. So much. "I've only known him a week."

"Sometimes it just takes a second. A heartbeat."

Katherine watched Nick bury his face against Kayla's tummy, tickling her, wrangling another of those gut laughs from the ten-month-old that were so contagious.

She'd never experienced love with a man first-hand before, but given how she'd come alive when she'd met Nick, how he made her knees weak and her heart soar, she knew she'd been inflicted now.

But if that was true, could she somehow convince this man, who'd lived his entire life without love, that it could work for him?

And if she did…what then? Her life was in Seattle, a world away from here.

His world was here, right here.

He'd never leave.

That left her being the one to move… A week was one thing, but could she walk away from everything and everyone she'd ever known and be happy here forever?

No doubt. Truthfully, she didn't consider geographical issues a deterrent to true love, to a deep and meaningful relationship such as the kind she wanted with Nick. Their living in separate states wasn't what would hold them back.

Nope, it was the little matter of her wanting to be loved. Loved beyond anything she'd ever known. Loved like in her fantasies.

Living here with Nick and his daughters wouldn't work for her under any other conditions.

In the middle of twirling his daughters around on his back, Nick stopped and looked over at her, red bite on his neck and all. "Come here. I need another back."

Leila raised a brow, any wariness and lingering anxiety gone. "You're wanted."

She was. And if her heart hadn't already swelled from everything the past few days had brought, it did now, threatening to burst. With a grin, she leaped into the fray.

LEILA WENT BACK to her sister's, with the promise to come back for a little while each day to give Nick and Katherine time alone if they desired.

They desired.

And Katherine desired so much more on top of that. She was on a mission now, to show Nick how good love could be in his life, if he'd only give it a chance.

That she was thinking along these lines at all made her breath catch if she contemplated it too long. So she didn't, she just…enjoyed.

And dreamed.

That night they put the girls to bed together. Emily, the warrior princess, went without a whimper, asleep before she hit the pillow. Annie's head kept nodding, but then she'd jerk upright, clearly fighting to stay awake.

"Go to sleep," Nick whispered, and kissed her.

"No sleep." Stubborn to the end, she blinked furiously. "Daddy! My eyes are closing!"

"Because you're tired," he said with only a little patience. "Let them close, Annie. For God's sake, give in."

"But…" She sighed, and her eyes fell shut for the last time.

On the other side of the room, Katherine was having a hard time letting go of the warm and cuddly Kayla, who was ready to be put into her crib. The baby's warm little body lay so trustingly in her arms, and she smelled like powder and soft, wonderful infant—

"She's asleep," Nick said in Katherine's ear, letting out a long breath as he rubbed his jaw against hers, setting off delicious shivers down her spine. "They all are. Do you have any idea what a miracle that is? Hurry, we might actually have some time to ourselves." Leaning in, he kissed the top of Kayla's head. "Set her down, she'll be fine."

Yes, but would Katherine? It hadn't taken Kayla's and Emily's receptive, open little hearts long to latch onto her, and it had taken even less time for Katherine to latch onto them.

"You're thinking too much again," Nick said, and took Kayla from her arms, settling the baby in her crib with a gentleness that belied the sheer size of him.

Then he took Katherine's hand and led her down the hall, into his bedroom. He shut the door firmly behind him. His gaze dark and intent on hers, he locked it, the click of the tumbler sliding into place echoing in the silent room, intensifying the intimacy of what the sound meant.

He wanted her again.

Her heart jerked.

Leaning back against the door, he removed one boot, let it fall to the floor. "Did you talk to Alexandra? Everything good?" His other boot hit the floor, and then his socks, and he straightened, hands on the buttons of his Levi's.

"Alexandra is a bit of a wreck." As she watched him, her insides went soft and pliant, and it wasn't purely physical, though she had to admit, she wasn't going to take her eyes off him as he undid those buttons one by one. He tugged off his shirt then, exposing his broad chest and sinewy shoulders and arms. There was a light spattering of dark hair from pec to pec, and then one line bisecting his tight, flat belly, vanishing into his open jeans.

Shockingly, she wanted to follow that line with her lips.

"Did she put the plans into motion for that benefit auction?" Balling up his shirt, he tossed it across the room.

"Yeah, she—" He shoved off his jeans and

shorts, all in one motion, and when he kicked them away, he was gloriously nude.

And aroused.

"She what?" he asked.

It took her a moment to remember they were having a conversation. An important one. "She said Jordan Edwards's memorial isn't going to be until next weekend, so I won't miss it. And..."

He came toward her, tugged her close. Lifting her up, he set her down on his great, big bed and started working on her boots. When they'd both hit the floor, he reached for her shirt. "And..." he coaxed, tossing her shirt in the same direction as his clothes.

"And Hannah is due back to work t-tomorrow—" she stuttered as he unhooked her bra, slid it off her arms and cupped her breasts in his hands. "Sh-she'll be able to help—"

He let out a hum of acknowledgement and his fingers rasped over her nipples. "Does it make you feel better knowing that?" He unzipped her pants, slipped his hands inside and pulled her against him. "Because I'm all for helping make you feel better."

She sighed with pleasure. Being with him, breathing him in, feeling his heat and strength wrap around her, she came alive. She always did when he touched her. "I'm feeling better...yes, lots better. Nick..."

Surging up to his knees, he worked her jeans and

panties down. "Yeah?" He ran his hands up her legs until they met at the juncture.

With a gasp, she arched her hips. "I don't like to think about going back."

"So don't." He lifted her up to straddle him, one hand tight against her buttocks, holding her in place, the other on her breast. "Stay here with me." He rocked her against him.

She struggled to keep her train of thought. "I...have to go back."

"So go fix everything, and then come back here." He pushed her back on the bed, grabbed a condom from his nightstand drawer and looked at her as he put it on. "It seems easy enough..." His gaze ran down her body and he let out a rumbling breath of hunger. Then he wrapped a fist around his erection, guiding himself to her hot center.

One stroke and he was deep inside, and her thoughts scattered because he filled her like no one else ever had, filled her from the inside out.

"What do you think?" He towered over her, slipping his hands beneath her thighs, groaning his encouragement when she wrapped them around his waist. "Go to the memorial..." He sighed as he slowly stroked her once. "Work out the loan issues, then come back."

"I...what about the day care?"

"Open a new one." His second thrust scooted her

up on the bed and she dug her fingers into his tight butt. "Or don't." He panted for breath and thrust again. "Just come back and be with me."

Be with him. God, did he have any idea how wonderful that sounded? How much she wanted it?

Then he thrust again, deeper, harder, and she lost the ability to think beyond what he was doing to her. She clung to him, her entire body quickening, tightening as he drove into her, demanding all her attention, commanding her body, her senses. She was panting for breath, writhing and whimpering and begging before he finally allowed her release and sent her skittering off the edge.

He followed.

*"Jesus,"* he breathed after long moments of simply lying on top of her, a welcome weight.

He turned his head and brushed his lips against her temple. "You wreck me. You completely wreck me."

"Nick—"

"Even as you make me whole."

She went still.

Wished she could see his face.

Then he slid off her to his side and propped himself up on an elbow, settling one hand low on her belly, keeping her close.

Letting her see his face, and anything else she wanted to see.

She knew that she'd just been given more from him in the way of words than he'd ever given before, and she slid her arms around him, curling close.

He pulled the blanket up over them, hugging her tight as he let out a long breath. "My eyes are closing, Kat," he whispered with a smile in his drowsy voice.

Her fingers drifted over his face, and when he sighed with pleasure, with sleep, she sighed, too.

## CHAPTER FOURTEEN

THE NEXT DAY, Katherine called Alexandra to check in.

"Hannah's back and looking rested and healthy," Alexandra said of their third partner.

Katherine laughed. "I'm so glad."

"She's also keeping a secret."

"What do you mean?"

"I don't know really, just a hunch. She went to her mother's house and was helping organize stuff for a garage sale. She found a small hand-carved box with a packet of her mother's letters in it. Whatever was in them upset her. You'll have to try to get it out of her when you get back."

"Okay." But Katherine was sidetracked with the thought...*what if I don't come back?*

"And I don't want you to feel guilty about this, but Carlos came home. They got rained out. I've got him here and he's fine and he's going to be perfectly happy with me until you get back."

"Oh, Alexandra—"

"It's no imposition, we're going to have a ball.

Don't give it another thought. Hold on though, he's dying to talk to you.''

Then Carlos was on the phone, talking at his usual one hundred miles per hour. ''We had so much fun in the rain,'' he said. ''There was mud everywhere and the boys nailed the girls in a mud fight, but the teachers thought it was too wet—how can rain be too wet?—and they made us come home.''

''I'm sorry, baby. I know you wanted to camp the whole week—''

''It's all right. Alexandra's place is cool, and she made pizza... But I have lots of homework, which isn't really fair cuz when we were camping, there wasn't homework. Alexandra took me home to get a book I needed and I grabbed the mail while I was there and...'' He slowed down. Whispered. ''There's something from the state.''

''I went and met with them before I came up here, remember? Probably more forms for me to sign.''

''Yeah.''

He didn't sound convinced, and she wanted to hug him. ''Open the envelope, sweetie.''

''Are you sure?''

''Of course.''

She heard paper rip, then his low murmured voice as he read the words to himself.

''What is it?'' she asked.

He was quiet for a moment, and when he spoke, his voice quivered. ''It's more forms, but the letter says everything looks in order so far. There's going to be the required hearing next month. I guess I'm…almost yours.''

Tears sprang to her eyes, both at the news, and the emotion in his voice. ''Oh, sweetie…this is celebration-worthy news. I can't wait to hug you. I love you, Carlos.''

''Love you, too…*Mom.*''

She laughed as a few of the tears ran down her cheeks. ''I really miss you.''

''Yeah. So are you coming back…or am I making an address and school change?''

Katherine looked out the window at the incredible view of the Alaskan mountains. She thought of how much he'd love it here. ''You'll be the first to know, right after I sort it all out.''

''Is there a lot of sorting left to do?''

''I'm not sure,'' she whispered, and wished she was. ''It's all so complicated.''

''Why?''

She opened her mouth to list all the reasons why, and found she couldn't come up with one. It made her laugh. ''I'll call you tomorrow, okay? Be good.''

''I will if you will.''


THEY SPENT the day in Anchorage, Katherine, Nick and the three girls. They took the plane, landing at the small, private airport where it had all begun for Nick, at Paddy's.

Nick smiled at the high school kid who came out to help him tie down. "Hey, Kyle."

Kyle grinned, knowing Nick used to have his job years before, and also knowing Nick was a generous tipper. "Fuel her up, Nick?"

"Yep." He helped Kat and the girls out of the plane, and Annie squealed at the sight of Kyle.

"Piggyback!" she demanded, making Kyle laugh.

"Not now, squirt," he said with a fond smile. "After I fuel up, though, okay?"

Annie pouted until he relented and put her on his back.

"*Candy,*" she demanded next, and Kyle looked at Nick.

"Only one candy bar this time," he said, and handed Kyle ten bucks and a grinning Emily, too. "I'll meet you in Paddy's office."

Nick turned back for Kat, who was holding Kayla. The baby had one chubby arm around Kat's neck, and her head on her shoulder, looking up at Kat with sleepy-eyed adoration, and for a moment, his heart tugged hard.

"She's tired," Kat said. "She'd just started to fall asleep— Nick? What is it?"

He shook his head. He wouldn't burden her with the knowledge that Kayla had bonded with her like she'd bonded with no one before. Nor would he burden her with something else—*he'd* bonded as well.

He didn't want to influence her decision to stay with any guilt trips. "You're beautiful," he said, and meant it.

"Oh…" She gave him a dreamy smile. "So are you."

He took her inside to meet Paddy, and found the sixty-eight-year-old beneath a twin-engine Baron, with only his scarred boots sticking out. They were tapping to the country music on the radio. "Hey, old man. What does it take to get some service around here?"

The boots went still. "It takes three darlin' little women, which you'd better have brought with you." Paddy scooted himself out from beneath the plane. "You were supposed to bring them by last week, you no good son of a—" Flat on his back on a roller, Paddy blinked up at Katherine in surprise and chagrin. *"Oops."*

"I brought you *four* 'darlin' women this time. Katherine Kinard, meet Paddy McQuintle."

Paddy rolled to his knees, and Nick leaned down to give him a hand up. His bones creaked as he stood. "Hear that? I'm getting old."

Paddy had been saying he was getting old for over twenty years. He wiped a hand on his jeans, then thrust it at Kat. "Nice to meet you. And you…" he cooed to Kayla, touching her nose, making the little girl give him a toothless smile. "There's my dar-lin'."

"Paddy, Paddy!" Annie came running back into the hangar with Kyle and Emily just behind her. She threw herself at Paddy, and when he lifted her, he smiled into her chocolate-covered face. "Kyle's taking good care of you then?"

"Yes. You should give him a lift."

Kyle winced. "Raise. He should give me a *raise*."

"Raise," Annie repeated dutifully.

Paddy laughed.

Kyle blushed.

Emily waddled over to Paddy and tugged on his jeans. He put down Annie and picked up Emily.

"Hey," Annie complained, and stomped her foot.

"Hay is for horses." Paddy rubbed noses with Emily's equally chocolate-covered face. Then he set Emily down too, and looked at Katherine. "So he did it, he actually brought back a wife. You know what you're in for, Katherine Kinard?"

Nick opened his mouth but Kat smiled. "I didn't marry him."

He frowned. "Why not?"

"Well, because—"

"Because he's a catch, young lady, I'll tell you that. If I was thirty years younger, and a chick, I'd marry him in a heartbeat."

Katherine laughed. "Well, then, lucky for me you're not." She smiled at Nick. "I've come for a visit. I've never seen Alaska."

"Now you've seen it," Paddy said. "You going to marry him now?"

Nick slipped an arm around Kat's waist. "That's it, scare her off before I've convinced her."

Looking a little sheepish, Paddy scratched his head. "Sorry."

"It's okay," Kat said softly. "I think it's incredibly sweet how much you want Nick taken care of." She squeezed his hand, letting out another smile, and won Paddy over with ease.

"Can I leave the plane here for a while?" Nick asked.

Paddy lifted a brow. "Just bring me back a burger from Jo's."

THEY WENT SHOPPING and milling around Anchorage for a few hours, which turned out to be far more city than Katherine could have imagined.

Lunch was at a little café called Jo's, run by a woman who could have been Leila's twin.

Turns out she was, and Jo treated Nick much the same as her sister did, with a mixture of annoyed affection. It was a mom-and-pop place that had seen better days, with scarred linoleum floors, harsh fluorescent lights and tables with matchbooks beneath a leg or two to keep them steady. The wallpaper was faded and the waitresses chomped gum and were heavy with attitude, but Katherine loved it. The windows were frosted, and the customers dressed ruggedly as Alaskans tended to, and she sat there surrounded by Nick and the girls and felt like a local, eating food that turned out to be nothing short of mouthwatering.

By the time they headed back to Paddy with the promised burger and flew home, the girls were in heaven from their day out, and Katherine had to say, she felt the same.

She really did love it here, and could easily, so easily it was a bit shocking, imagine herself here, opening a day care, loving life and never looking back.

Forrester Square Day Care 2... The idea wasn't that far-fetched. She could actually see herself doing it.

Nick had been a great host, and if she got the feeling he was trying to make sure she saw Anchorage as a replacement for Seattle, if he wanted to show her the city had culture and excitement and an array of things to do and see, he'd succeeded.

But it hadn't taken today to get attached to the place, or his girls. She'd done that on first sight.

Same as for him.

THE NEXT DAY when Leila showed up to give them several hours alone, Nick took Kat out in his canoe, down the river to one of his favorite spots, where it widened into a perfect natural pool.

Annie couldn't wait to swim here this summer, and he had a fantasy about Kat swimming there, too.

Swimsuit not required.

They lay on the shore and talked about his work, which he'd put off last week and desperately needed to get back to. They talked about her day-care center, and the ongoing plans for the benefit to save it. Alexandra continued to call every day, filling her in, and Nick was grateful, because without that contact, he was certain Kat would have gone home.

He wasn't ready for that, not when he hadn't yet convinced her to come back.

They talked about how much he loved flying, how it appealed to his need for wide-open space and freedom.

And then they talked about the past few nights they'd spent lost in each other's arms, and their passion.

"I've never had anyone do all the things to me that you've done," she admitted softly.

He came up on his elbow, looking into her face as he twirled a strand of her hair between his fingers. "Like what?"

"Like...like when you licked me from head to toe." She let out a breathless laugh. "That I liked. I liked that a lot."

Just thinking about it now made him hard. "You did, huh?"

"Oh, yes."

"Good." He stripped them both down to the skin and did everything in his power to show her that he liked it, too, that she could have anything she wanted, all she needed to do was ask.

Oh, and stay.

THE NEXT DAY Nick had to fly mail and supplies out to several outposts, and couldn't cancel no matter how badly he wanted to, so he left Katherine with the girls.

There was some guilt to that, even knowing she was a teacher and loved his kids—

No, that was just an excuse on his part. She was made for such a thing, she had a heart so full it seemed to have no boundaries.

It was his deal, his guilt, because he wanted to spend as much time with her as possible.

Before she left.

He ended up being gone twice as long as he'd planned. A woman in labor needed a ride to Anchorage, and then a fly fisherman offered to pay him triple for a ride.

When he finally got home hours later, he didn't know what to expect. Kat in a straitjacket, maybe, but the house was light and warm, and his four women were in the kitchen.

Each daughter except Kayla—fast asleep in her carrier—was white from head to toe, covered in flour.

"We made cookies," Annie said proudly as he kissed each of the girls.

"We even saved you some," Kat said, also covered in flour, also adorable.

Sexy adorable. He wanted to eat her right up. And given the way she looked at him right back, all soft and dewy and hopeful, she knew it. "Did you have a good day?" she whispered against his lips when he kissed her, too.

"Better now."

THEY DIDN'T GET much sleep that night, but not because of the kids. Knowing there were only two days left before she was going back kept him up for hours, and because he was selfish, he kept her up, as well, worshipping her body, letting her worship his.

The next day they all spent together. He took them up in his plane for some sightseeing Alaska-style. Or "eyeing" as Emily called it.

"Eye, Daddy," she squealed, lifting her arms like a bird as they took off. "Eye!"

"Yes, Emmie, we're flying," Nick said, and shook his head.

"Faster, Daddy," Annie directed hopefully. *"Faster."*

Kayla pumped her legs and sucked on her fist and cooed, already well used to the heady feeling as they rose in the sky.

"There," Nick said to Kat, pointing out Tar Inlet in Glacier Bay. "Those natural sculptures are ice drifts, shed by a glacier."

She stared down at the ice formations sticking up out of the water. "They're beautiful. How old are they?"

"Centuries."

"My God." She kept her face pressed against the window, soaking up the view he'd wanted her to see. He'd wanted to show her his world, and this was a huge part of it.

"Oh, Nick," she breathed, and glanced over at him. "It's all so…incredible."

"Yeah." At her words, he felt the fist around his heart loosen slightly. It had been there since she'd first flown into this world from hers. "Within this national park, there's sixteen glaciers that descend directly into the sea. Look—" He pointed to a series of large black animals moving on a shore far below. "Harbor seals."

"They're adorable!" she cried. "Look, girls, do you see them?"

Emily and Annie pressed their noses to the glass, as well, oohing and aahing over the sights with her.

"Land the plane, Daddy," Annie demanded. "I want to pet a seal."

Nick laughed. "Not this time." He spent the next hour flying over the spectacles of the glaciers below, the unforgettable glimpses of wildlife—thousands of puffins sunning on rocks, two black bears sitting together in a meadow chomping on wild berries...everything he could to make Kat see this world as he did.

And to want to stay.

AFTER DINNER, they had ice-cream sundaes, and when they finally got the girls to bed, Nick grabbed the chocolate sauce in one hand and Katherine in the other.

"What are you doing?" she asked breathlessly, a look of sexy anticipation on her face.

"You'll see." He took her into his room. "Get on the bed, Kat. No clothes."

"Um...okay." Laughing a little, she stripped down. "Are you trying to make me nervous, because—" This ended in a gasp when he squeezed a line of chocolate syrup over her breasts. Her nipples hardened, and so did he.

"Nick...what are you doing?"

"Having dessert." He dribbled a line down her quivering belly. "Open your legs, Kat— God. Yeah, like that." And he dribbled chocolate there, too.

Kat gasped again.

Nick tossed the bottle over his shoulder and kneeled on the bed, staring down at the feast waiting for him. Then he lowered his mouth and began to lick it off.

"N-Nick."

"Mmm...yeah?" He lifted his head to find her eyes glazed over.

"You're next," she managed.

THE NEXT DAY Nick woke up with Kat in his arms and a smile on his face.

Until he remembered...his week was nearly up. Only one more night.

He'd better make it count.

# CHAPTER FIFTEEN

KATHERINE SPENT her last full day with Nick and the girls, hiking, catching tadpoles, and picking wildflowers. It was a day she'd never forget.

That evening, Nick rushed the girls through their dinner and baths. He'd gotten Leila to baby-sit, but when Katherine asked why, he'd only say he had a surprise for her, and that she should dress as she would for a night out on the town in Seattle.

So she put on the only dress she'd brought with her. Long and flowery, with a row of tiny, delicate buttons down the front, she loved it for its forgiving cut, since it made her feel pretty.

Or maybe that was the look in Nick's eyes when she came into the living room after getting ready.

He'd been making a fire, but he went still for a beat, then stood up and walked toward her. "Wow."

"I take it you like the dress," she said with a smile.

With his gaze locked on hers, he sank his fingers into her hair at the nape of her neck, tugging gently until her face was turned up. Then he kissed her.

Still looking deep into her eyes, he pulled back only slightly. "What I like," he said, "is you. The dress, however, is a fine bonus."

She laughed, suspecting he'd meant her to. But the tension was still there. It had been all day.

She was going home. Tomorrow morning.

"We don't have to go out tonight, Nick. We can just…" Go to bed, she was thinking, but he shook his head.

"Out," he insisted.

They drove into Anchorage this time, through beautiful winding roads, glowing by the light of the moon. A wordless anticipation rose in the car. Katherine wondered at it, at what he was up to, and if it would involve putting words to his feelings.

He'd all but shown her how he felt so many times over the past few days, and she hoped to God he meant it, because every minute she spent with him, she fell a little harder.

He pulled up at Jo's, the small café where they'd had lunch the other day with the girls. Helping her out of his truck, Nick used the opportunity to haul her against him, planting a thorough kiss that left her breathless and humming with pleasure.

"No more of that," he muttered, "or we'll never make it." He grabbed her hand and started toward the restaurant. He stopped at the door. Blocking her view when she tried to peer inside, he shifted his weight and looked the most unsure she'd ever seen him. "You came to Alaska, for me." His fingers ran over her jaw. "Do you have any idea how much that means to me?"

She reached up and covered his fingers with her own, bringing them to her heart. "Oh, Nick."

"I know that being here isn't like being in your big city, but I wanted to give you something back." Eyes on hers, he opened the door behind him.

The first thing she noticed was the softly lit dining room. Candles flickered from each table, in all the windows, and along the countertops. The center table had an ivory tablecloth and had been decorated with beautiful china and silverware, and a lovely centerpiece made from red roses and baby's breath.

No one was in the place.

"Pretend it's a big city restaurant," he said in her ear. "One that doesn't serve sushi."

"You did this for me?" She turned in a slow circle, taking it all in without the harsh fluorescent lighting, the rough edges softened by the candles.

"To make you feel at home."

She laughed even as her chest ached. "You can't do that with a fancy tablecloth and a few candles."

He stared at her, baffled.

"Do you want to know what I need to feel at home, Nick?"

"Seattle?"

"No."

He was looking at her in utter confusion, so sexy and unraveled that she slipped her arms around his neck and brushed up close. "You," she whispered.

He let out a low laugh. "I like the sound of that, I like it a lot, but..." He blinked into the unshed tears shimmering in her eyes. "What are you doing?"

"Kissing you." She went up on tiptoe and tried to put her mouth to his, but he held her back and peered into her face.

"You're crying," he accused, clearly terrified at the thought. *"Why?"*

"Haven't you ever been so happy you cry?"

"No."

She gently fought his hands and brushed her lips over his, and felt him tense. She did it again with a little sigh.

"Well, now, *there's* a reaction I can handle," he murmured, and caught her up, straightening so that her toes left the floor. His mouth came down on hers in a long, hungry, soul-searching kiss.

When he lifted his head, she pulled his mouth back to hers. She didn't want to talk about her tears, or anything else. Slowly, taking him with her, she backed to the table and pulled herself up on it. "Here, Nick?" she asked, as she had on the mountain that first time. "Now?"

He let out a groan. "Kat."

She started to lie back, but with a rough grumble in his chest, he stopped her. "This kills me, but Jo's in the back. Cooking."

"Oh." She laughed and hopped off the table. "Not here then. Not now."

"Later," he promised in a voice that had a thrilling shiver race down her spine. "But first..." He grimaced. "Okay, listen. Leila told me to be...romantic, and we all know how good I am at that."

Her throat tightened again. "I think you're better than you know."

"Yeah, so good I have you in tears."

"Oh, Nick. I—"

"I just thought you might think of Alaska as your home if it looked more like—"

"I don't need Alaska to look like anything other than what it is." She gestured around her at the candles, the flowers. "This is beautiful, Nick, but truthfully? I just want to be with you."

That seemed to make him speechless.

"Trust me," she whispered. "*You* make me feel at home. *You* make me happy. *You* make me feel good. When I'm with you, I feel whole and alive. And what you did for me tonight, trying to give me what you think I want...well, just thinking about it puts a big dopey smile on my face." She moved closer so they were toe-to-toe, and wrapped her arms around him. "Every moment of every day we spend together, whether it's on the mountain or in your house…I feel at home. And that's because of you. I don't need fancy silver and fragile china. All I need is you." She smiled. "*There*. A whole bunch of words when you needed to hear them. Now I need to hear some." She squeezed him and straightened, still smiling at him through her lingering tears when he just stared at her. "Your turn," she said gently. *Please.*

He opened his mouth, then closed it.

"You wanted me happy," she whispered. "And I am. You wanted me to feel at home with you. Well, I do. But I don't know how you feel about me, or us, and I want to. I can guess, and I like what I'm guessing, but I really need the words from you. I just do."

"I want you to stay."

"Yes," she said. "I know those words. You want a wife, though you'd like it different this time from last time, with more passion…and less pain. You want a mother for your children, and I understand that, believe me. They deserve that. But you deserve something too, Nick. You deserve love and happiness, too."

"I don't need—"

"Everyone needs," she said softly, her heart

breaking that he still didn't see that, or if he did, wasn't ready to admit it. "Everyone—" She broke off with a long breath when the cell phone in his pocket rang.

He didn't move.

"Aren't you going to get that?" she asked.

"I want to finish this."

She imagined he did. As a commitmentphobic, he wanted to finish it and move on and never discuss it again. "Answer the phone," she said. "I'm not going anywhere."

"It's the house," he said when he'd checked the display, and lifted the phone to his ear. "What's the matter?" He listened for a moment, his jaw going tight enough to invoke a muscle tic. "How long ago?" He nodded. "No, don't go out there with the two little ones, we'll be right back." He clicked off, looked at her. "Annie vanished on Leila. The back door's ajar so Leila has a good idea where she went."

"My God! Where?"

"I'll have to show you," he said grimly, and stood up. "I'm sorry, we have to go."

"Of course. Did she call the police?"

"We'll get there faster than they will." He ran with her to the truck. "Besides, I know where she is."

BREAKING JUST ABOUT every speed limit, Nick got them home in record time. He ran straight through the house and into the kitchen, where Leila was pacing with a fretting Kayla in her arms. "I called and called her," Leila said. "Stubborn girl won't come."

Emily sat on the floor with a box of crayons and a pad of paper, her face screwed up in a frown. Her fingers were very busy as she sat there systematically breaking every crayon in the box.

Nick looked down at the obviously upset Emily and shoved his fingers through his hair. "Emmie, I know where she is, I'm going to go get her right now, okay?"

Emily broke another crayon.

Nick squatted in front of her and gathered her close for a hug. "I'll be right back, baby. Don't break all the crayons. We'll color, okay?"

Emily tipped her head up for a kiss, and feeling his heart tighten in his chest, he gave it to her. "Be right back," he whispered, then turned to Kat.

He had no right to ask her to comfort his children, to help him out, but he was going to ask anyway. And yet before he could so much as open his mouth, she'd taken Kayla from Leila, and cuddled her close. Then, still in her pretty dress, she sat on his kitchen floor and pulled Emily into her lap, too. "I've got them," she said to him. "Go bring her back."

He stood there staring down at his entire world and wanted to say something, anything, but "thank you" seemed woefully inadequate and nothing else came to him in his distraction over Annie. So he whipped around and headed out the back door.

It was an unusually warm spring night, thank God, with a half moon that lit his way. Still, his heart thundered in his chest as he took the narrow path from the house off to the left, through a thicket of pine trees and to a clearing.

The small fenced-in garden was Cassandra's memorial, which he'd built for the girls. Annie loved to sit in the middle of the wildflowers and talk to her.

The little girl of his heart was there now, huddled in a tiny ball, her thin arms wrapped around her legs, staring miserably off into the night.

"Annie." Taking his first good breath since Leila's call, he let himself in the gate.

She didn't even look his way.

Though the ground was wet, he sank to the earth next to her and hauled her into his lap. He buried his face in her thick, long hair and wondered what the hell was going to come of them. "Even though I knew where you'd gone, you scared me."

"I can't see Momma anymore."

He lifted his head and looked into her tear-streaked face. "What?"

"I can't remember what she looked like."

"We have pictures of her everywhere. You have one right there in your locket." He lifted the chain she wore around her neck and opened the heart locket to show her. "See?"

Annie stared down at her mother's smiling face and her eyes filled. "I can see her now, but when I close my eyes…" She closed her eyes. More tears leaked out. "I can't." She opened huge, dark eyes on Nick. "I used to see her when I wanted, and now she's going away."

"Oh, baby." Heart breaking, he hugged her close. "Maybe you can't see her like you want to, but she still lives in your heart."

"But I want her to live outside my heart. I want her to live in our house again."

"I know." He rocked her back and forth. Stroking her slim spine, she felt so little and fragile. "I know."

"Did she comb my hair?"

"Whether you wanted it combed or not."

"Did she tell me to brush my teeth?"

He smiled. "Oh, yeah."

"Did she hug me?"

"Lots."

She was quiet for a while. Then she looked right at him. "Kat does all those things for me."

Nick stroked his thumb over a lingering tear on her cheek. "I know."

"Kayla doesn't remember Mommy. Kayla thinks Kat is her mommy."

"Kayla is very young, Annie. She—"

"Emily doesn't remember Mommy. And when she fell down today, she wanted Kat."

"She's only two, and—"

"I know. But Kat's leaving."

"Yes."

"Maybe you should keep her here—don't take her home in the morning."

"You don't just keep someone, Annie." Nick had to smile, though he felt like he'd swallowed a football. "They have to want to stay."

"Kat wants to stay. I know it. She said…"

"She said what?"

Annie leaned her head back on his arm and studied the dark sky littered with brilliant stars. "She said she loved everything here. So that means she loves me and Emmie and Kayla." She looked at Nick. "And you, Daddy. She loves you."

"You think so, huh?"

"Yes. And Emmie and Kayla need her."

"How about you?"

"I'm too big. I don't need anyone."

Oh boy. A chip right off the old block. "You know, it's okay to let someone else inside your heart,'' he said. ''Your mom...she'd understand, Annie. She really would.''

''Are you going to let Kat in your heart?''

Nick looked at Annie. ''How old are you again?''

''Four going on thirty.''

He laughed. That's what he always told her.

''So why can't we keep Kat?''

Nick put his forehead to hers. ''Maybe I can work on that.''

''Leila says you are working on it.''

''I think,'' he said, surging to his feet with Annie still in his arms, ''that I just realized how I can work on that a little harder.''

''Kay.'' She yawned wide and set her head on his shoulder.

Damn, he loved this kid. ''What do you say we go back to the house and see what they're doing without us?''

She flung her arms around his neck and nodded. ''Emily probably broke something. Or ate it.''

''Probably.''

''Kayla probably drooled over everything.''

''No doubt.''

Around them, the night was noisy. Crickets singing. Wind blowing lightly, making all the spring growth rustle.

Halfway back, Annie stirred in his arms. ''Daddy?''

"Yeah?"

She snuggled in closer. "I love you."

The L-word again. Were all the females in his life born with it on the tip of their tongues?

"Daddy? Did you hear me? I said I love you."

"I love you, too, baby." Hell if he didn't love all of them—her and Emily and Kayla.

And...and quite possibly one Katherine Kinard, as well.

Why was it so easy to say it to his daughter and not her? He knew damn well Kat loved him back, that it was a real and binding and deep sort of love. Just thinking it made him stumble.

Christ, he'd been a fool, withholding those three words from her. Obviously she'd seen it in his eyes, seen how he felt. He could tell by the way she looked at him in return, how everything about her softened. He could tell by the way she touched him, as if he was her entire life.

The truth was, she'd given him everything he'd asked for. She'd dropped her own life to come here with him, she'd loved his children as if they were her own and she'd fit in without effort.

And all she'd asked for in return were the words to the feelings in his heart.

He was a fool.

But even a fool could change his ways. He started moving again, faster now. His house came into view, lighting up the night like a welcome beacon, and as always, he felt lighter of spirit just entering the place he'd built by himself.

Leila took one look at Annie and burst into tears. "I'm too old for this," she sobbed into her apron.

Kat set the sleepy Kayla into her baby carrier and Emily down near her crayons and gave Leila a hug. "It's okay, everything's okay."

"I knew where she'd gone, but still, anything could have happened to her—"

"I know, but see…" She pulled back and smiled when Leila looked around the room. "Nothing did happen to her. We're all here, safe and sound."

"I like the sound of that we," Leila said.

"I do, too." With a last hug, Katherine moved away from Leila and came toward Nick and Annie.

Patting Annie very gently on the back until the little girl looked at her, she smiled. "Hi, Annie."

"Hi, Kat."

Kat let out a sound halfway between a laugh and a sob. "I'm so very, *very* happy to see you, sweetheart. Are you all right now?"

"I went to the place where my mommy used to plant flowers. Daddy put a gate around it and told me I could go there anytime I wanted."

Kat nodded solemnly. "I bet it was beautiful by moonlight."

"I wanted to see her, but I couldn't."

"Oh, sweetie. Did you look in your heart? That's where she is, she's right there all the time."

"That's what my daddy said." Annie smiled. "Is my daddy in your heart all the time, too?"

## CHAPTER SIXTEEN

AT ANNIE'S QUESTION, Kat looked over at Nick. At all he saw in her eyes, his heart stopped.

"Is he?" Annie repeated in all her four-year-old impatience. "Is my daddy in your heart?"

Kat's smile was slow and tender. "Oh, yes," she breathed.

"Are you in his?" Annie demanded.

Kat cocked her head to the side and studied Nick some more. "You know what? I think I am."

"Kat—"

Emily stopped him cold with a bloodcurdling scream. They all whipped around to look at her, sitting on the floor with her finger on her nose, a blue crayon in her other hand, missing its tip.

Nick thrust Annie at Kat and reached for Emily. Holding her up, he stared into her horrified, screaming face. "Did you eat that tip?"

Still screaming, she shook her head.

"Emily Leanne, tell me that crayon tip is *not* up your nose."

She scrunched up her face and continued to wail at a pitch that could break glass.

"Oh my God," Leila said, and crossed herself.

*"Jesus,"* Nick muttered, then rushed with her to the sink.

Katherine was stunned, as well. She'd been taking care of kids for years, and a crayon tip up the nose was a new one for her.

Nick used his finger to pinch the clear side of Emily's nose closed. "Blow," he demanded, holding her over the sink. "Blow hard."

Emily stopped screaming and blew.

The tip of the crayon hit the steel with a "clink."

Emily stopped screaming and stared at it, then burst out in her contagious laugh. "Oooh," she said, pointing to the offending tip of the crayon. "Bad. Verrrry bad."

Nick sagged a little. "Yeah, bad crayon." He rolled his eyes at Kat as he hugged the little girl close. Pulling back, he looked into Emily's face. "How many times have we discussed this? *Nothing* up your nose."

Emily put her finger in the aforementioned nose. "No nose."

Nick pulled her hand away and sighed. "That's right, nothing up your nose. Not even your finger. Got it?"

Emily smiled sweetly.

Nick looked around him at the chaos of the kitchen. Broken crayons scattered across the floor, dinner dishes in the sink from whatever Leila had fed the kids, mail across the table, probably loaded with bills.

He'd deal with it all tomorrow.

After he'd flown Kat home.

Heart heavy, he shifted Emily to his other arm and reached for Annie. "Bedtime."

"Daaaaad," Annie whined, making the word about fifteen syllables. "It's not time yet."

Nick looked at the clock. It was 8:29. "What time is your bedtime?"

"Eight-thirty. I have one more minute."

"It'll take that long to get you ready. Let's go."

"Do you want to be alone with Kat?"

KATHERINE LOOKED at Nick. So did everyone else.

"Yes," Nick said in a thrillingly frustrated voice, his gaze right on Katherine. "I just want to be alone with Kat."

"But I don't want to go to bed."

"Annie Marie, you're going to bed."

"But you have to tell her you want her in *your* heart, just like you said outside."

"*Annie.*" There was dire warning in his low voice, but his gaze never left Katherine, who suddenly couldn't breathe.

He'd said it, she thought. *He'd said he wanted her in his heart.*

"It's not a secret," Annie said, then looked around at the utter silence. "Right?"

"Leila." Nick sounded a bit desperate. "Could you—"

"Got it." She grabbed Kayla and Emily. "Let's go, Annie girl."

"I don't wanna."

Leila gently nudged the little girl in front of her, moving her out the door.

"But I wanna stay and listen—"

The kitchen door shut on her and Katherine stared at it, torn between laughter and anticipation and a sudden calm she couldn't believe. For whatever reason, everything was suddenly clear. "Nick," she said, still staring at the door. "I love your children." She looked at him. "I love your house and I love your world. But most of all, I love you."

He opened his mouth and she put her finger to his lips. "You make my heart feel like it's going to overflow, and that's my own little miracle."

"Kat—"

She tightened her finger over his mouth. "No," she whispered. "That was me just having to get it out. But you don't feel the same need, I know, and that's okay." She watched his eyes darken, feeling his hands, his big, warm hands, come up to squeeze her hips. God, she loved this man, so much. "Really. It's okay."

"Is it?" He took her hands and pulled them behind her back, which left her body snugged against his. "I learned something shocking tonight, Kat, and

I learned it from a four-year-old. Come on.'' He tugged her toward the back door.

The night had blossomed, and the sky dancing with brilliant stars in every hue and size, unlike anything she'd ever seen in the city. ''Oh,'' she breathed, soaking it in, the chilled air, the beauty of the spectacle without any lights detracting from it.

''Here,'' he said, and turning off the kitchen light, took her into the yard. Standing behind her, he wrapped his arms around her and set his chin on her head.

''I'd never get tired of this view—never,'' she whispered, and wrapped her arms around his, holding them tight to her middle, feeling surrounded by…love. Whether he said the words or not, she meant what she'd said. Just having him with her was enough.

''This evening didn't go the way I planned, Kat.''

''What did you plan?''

''To woo you senseless and then bring you back here. I'd have had you in bed by now, naked and panting my name.''

The cockiness of the statement made her laugh. ''Oh, really.''

''Really.'' He turned her around and touched her face with such tenderness she felt her heart constrict. ''But I find that much as I love having you naked and panting my name, there's something else I'd rather do with you tonight.''

"Our last night," she whispered.

He didn't say anything to that, just leaned in and kissed her softly, but when she moved in for more, he pulled back, running the pad of his thumb over her lower lip. "I don't have a lot of experience with letting people in," he said in a way that broke her heart. "I never lived with anyone related to me, and with no blood ties, I always felt...detached."

"Oh, Nick. I know."

"I had friends, and that was nice, but not soul deep, you know? No connections I had were soul deep, ever. Even when I got married."

"I know. Nick—"

He put his fingers over her lips this time. "And then the girls came, and they..." His eyes softened, a smile curved his lips. "They were amazing. And a part of me. A part of my heart." His smile deepened. "As my very smart daughter reminded me tonight. And you know what, Kat? I'd have sworn to you my heart was as full as it could get, that there was no more room—" He tightened his fingers on her mouth when she would have spoken. "But I was wrong. There is more room." He made the mistake of lifting his fingers from her mouth to haul her close.

"I love you, Nick," she whispered, unable to help herself.

"Now see, that's one of the things that drew me to you," he said, shaking his head. "You're your own woman. Meaning you can't follow directions and keep quiet when I'm trying to tell you something.''

''You love me back,'' she said, laughing. ''I know you do.''

''Yeah. I do.'' He let out a slow breath, dropped his hands from her and sank to the ground right there in the middle of the yard. He tipped his head up to her amused face. ''My knees feel weak and you're cracking up.''

She dropped to her knees beside him and tried to swallow her smile. ''Poor baby. So...I've really brought you to your knees?''

''Quite literally.''

His smile was absolutely disarming. Melting dark eyes, tanned rugged skin, long legs folded beneath him. Just looking at him made her weak, too. He was so devastatingly male, so sure of everything...except when it came to this. ''Nick—''

''You just won't let me say it—*I love you*,'' he said at last, reaching for her. ''I love you with everything I've got, Kat. Everything.'' He shot her an endearing, heartbreaking smile. ''Can you believe it?''

It wasn't a traditional heart-and-flowers thing, and he'd only dropped to his knees because it had been that or pass out, but it was real, and it was hers. True love at last. ''I believe it,'' she said. ''Now take me home.'' She rose to her feet and pulled him to his.

In the moonlight, he went a little pale. ''Kat—''

''This home, Nick. *Your* home.'' She nudged him backward, toward the house she'd fallen for as well as the man and his glorious three little girls. ''Take me inside and make me yours.''

''I will, gladly.'' He looked at the house. ''I know I'm sort of a package deal, and—''

''And I'm a package, too.''

''I want the whole enchilada,'' he said. ''Including Carlos.''

''And I want your whole package, Nick. The girls, the house, even Leila, if she wants to stay. I want all of you.''

''Forever?''

''Forever.''

''What about Seattle?''

She shrugged. ''You have a plane. You'll take me for visits, right?''

''Whenever you want to go.''

''So…make me yours.''

His smile was slow and full of promise. ''I've been waiting to hear you say that since the day you plowed into me.'' He slipped his arms around her and hauled her up against him.

She snaked her arms around his neck. ''So does this mean you'll teach me how to fly your plane?''

He went a little pale again. "Do you suppose you'll fly just like you drive?"

She grinned. "Probably."

He let out a low laugh. "Take my heart, take my kids, take my entire life…except the plane."

She bit his throat, and he laughed again, then she put her lips to the spot, and he groaned. "God, Kat, don't you know? You can have anything, anything at all, as long as you keep loving me. Even the damn plane. Take it all. Just don't ever leave."

Katherine closed her eyes, tipped her face back to the chilly night and felt a peace drape over her. Gone was the unsettling certainty that something was missing from her life. She had everything she wanted, in one fell swoop. "No, I won't ever leave," she whispered, and opened her eyes. "Not when everything I want is right here."

*FORRESTER SQUARE,*
*a new Harlequin series,*
*continues in June 2004 with*
Best-Laid Plans
*by Debbi Rawlins…*

After a painful divorce, Alana Fletcher and
her son, Corey, moved to Seattle for a fresh
start. Now Corey wanted to find his mom a
new husband—and to the six-year-old, Sean
Everett, the carpenter at his day care, was
perfect. But Alana made it clear that even *if*
she was looking, she'd want someone
more…settled…than Sean. Then an injury
caused Sean to suffer temporary amnesia—
and Corey saw his chance…

*Here's a preview!*

TWO DAYS OUT of the hospital and Sean still couldn't remember a damn thing. Not quite true. He did recall that he lived in Seattle and that he worked in construction, but he couldn't remember specifically where he lived or even that his name was really Sean Everett. He had to trust that he was being told the whole truth. The whole thing sucked.

Of course Alana was another story. He completely trusted her. Even though he had no specific memory, he felt their closeness, knew for certain they had some kind of connection. He wondered if they'd been dating before the accident. She'd only said that they were friends, but he had a feeling she was holding something back.

And Corey… Great kid. Always trying to be helpful. Sometimes too chatty, but Sean probably needed the noise. Otherwise, he thought too hard, and gave himself gigantic headaches.

"Sean, I'm home." Corey's voice rang from the kitchen, where he normally dumped his backpack when he got home from day care.

Another three seconds and his excited, flushed face appreared in the den. "Mom said we're having an early dinner because she has to go someplace tonight."

Sean's heart sank. The highlight of his day was spending time with Alana in the evening. Besides, he hated seeing her work all day and then having to cook and rush out again. "Hey, Corey, do you suppose I know how to cook?"

He nodded vigorously. "Better than Mom," he whispered, quickly checking over his shoulder.

Chuckling, Sean go to his feet. " We'll keep that our little secret." A sudden thought froze him to the spot. He already knew he'd fixed things around the house, that they were supposed to go fishing the Sunday after he'd had the accident. If he'd cooked for them, too...

He raked a hand through his hair, debating whether he should pump Corey for information. The kid talked a lot but didn't volunteer much...almost as if he'd been told not to. Sean cleared his throat. "So, I used to cook for you a lot, huh?"

Corey shrugged. "Sort of a lot."

"Was I around here much?"

Corey just stared at him with a slight frown.

"You know, kind of like I was your mom's boyfriend or something."

Corey blinked. An odd look crossed his face, and you could tell he was concentrating hard. Excitement sparkled in his eyes. You could almost see the wheels turning.

Sean ruffled his hair. "Hey, sport, what's going on?"

For a moment Corey was silent, then he flashed Sean a mischievous grin. "I'm not supposed to tell," he said, and pretended he was zipping his lips.

"Ah, I see." Sean made a show of thoughtfully scratching his jaw. "Well, now, I wouldn't want you to break any promises."

"I didn't promise nothing."

"But you aren't suppposed to tell?"

Corey shrugged. "I just can't let Mom know I told."

Sean hid a smile. He really shouldn't be a party to this... "I won't tell her if you won't."

Corey peeked behind him and then tugged at Sean's hand. Sean crouched down so that Corey could get close to his ear. "You aren't her boyfriend," he whispered excitedly. "You guys are married."

If you enjoyed what you just read,
then we've got an offer you can't resist!

# Take 2
# bestselling novels FREE!
# Plus get a FREE surprise gift!

Clip this page and mail it to The Best of the Best™

**IN U.S.A.**
3010 Walden Ave.
P.O. Box 1867
Buffalo, N.Y. 14240-1867

**IN CANADA**
P.O. Box 609
Fort Erie, Ontario
L2A 5X3

**YES!** Please send me 2 free Best of the Best™ novels and my free surprise gift. After receiving them, if I don't wish to receive anymore, I can return the shipping statement marked cancel. If I don't cancel, I will receive 4 brand-new novels every month, before they're available in stores! In the U.S.A., bill me at the bargain price of $4.74 plus 25¢ shipping and handling per book and applicable sales tax, if any*. In Canada, bill me at the bargain price of $5.24 plus 25¢ shipping and handling per book and applicable taxes**. That's the complete price and a savings of over 20% off the cover prices—what a great deal! I understand that accepting the 2 free books and gift places me under no obligation ever to buy any books. I can always return a shipment and cancel at any time. Even if I never buy another The Best of the Best™ book, the 2 free books and gift are mine to keep forever.

185 MDN DNWF
385 MDN DNWG

| Name | (PLEASE PRINT) | |
|---|---|---|
| Address | Apt.# | |
| City | State/Prov. | Zip/Postal Code |

\* Terms and prices subject to change without notice. Sales tax applicable in N.Y.
\*\* Canadian residents will be charged applicable provincial taxes and GST.
   All orders subject to approval. Offer limited to one per household and not valid to
   current The Best of the Best™ subscribers.
   ® are registered trademarks of Harlequin Enterprises Limited.

BOB02-R                                    ©1998 Harlequin Enterprises Limited

# Coming in May 2004 to Silhouette Books

When Jake Ingram is taken captive by the Coalition, a sexy undercover agent is sent to brainwash him. Though he finds her hard to resist, can he trust this mysterious beauty?

Five extraordinary siblings.

One dangerous past.

Unlimited potential.

**Look for more titles in this exhilarating new series, available only from Silhouette Books.**

Visit SilhouetteBooks at www.eHarlequin.com

FSCM

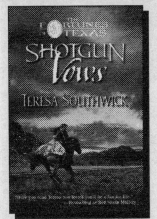

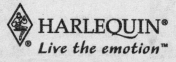